To

R. Sundar
and
S. Krishnan

North Star

- R.Chandramouli

Only birth can conquer death –

the birth not of the old thing again

but of something new.

Joseph Campbell

The Hero with the Thousand Faces

Title of the Book   - NORTH STAR
First Edition   - Augest 2009

ISBN : 978 -81 -87156 -57 -4

PRICE - Rs.190/-

Edited
by
V. Ramnarayan

Published
by
Think Big Books

an imprint of
S. Viswanathan (Printers & Publishers) Pvt. Ltd.
Old.No.38 (New No.6), Mc Nichols Road, Chetput,
Chennai - 600 031.
www.thinkbigbooks.in

Printed at
Bhavish Graphics, Chennai - 600 031.
www.bhavishgraphics.com

PROLOGUE

I recalled the order in which the dolls had to be stowed away in the attic. The earthen, painted dolls first, each swathed in cloth and hay, followed by the wax- moulded deities and the assortment of miniatures from the bottom-most rack. As the last of the dolls passed from hand to hand, and up a wooden ladder into their designated space in the attic, as the evening shadows descended on the skylight, the conclusion of the festivity became certain. Initial exuberance gave way to remorse. Silence engulfed the work environment. There was nothing more to stow away but the memories.

The youngest child broke into tears, the older ones gathered around me with downcast eyes, seeking restoration of a sense of purpose. I beckoned them to come closer, and hugged them tight, my outstretched arms encircling at least four. At that very moment, the physical bonding and emotional attachment must have enabled a transference of innocence, a simplicity of thought that dwells in us only during childhood. At that very moment, a fresh clarity dawned, not one as severe and sudden as the revelation sparked by the flamethrower, but a clairvoyance conveyed kinder and gentler, which in the days to come, could help resolve my constant conflicts with the past.

I realized at that moment the dolls served as a metaphor, and the act of putting them away symbolized the storage of memories in the safe repository of my heart. The stowage signified that the past would, and should never go away. Yet, the yesteryear can be wrapped and returned to where it belongs, in the attic of our soul, where memories of yore and yonder, of people and places, dwell in peace and harmony. The mystical helpers of our childhood reside within, and when we seek that which is lost, elfins, pixies and goblins emerge from the depository, to revive the romance of the nursery, rekindling the gentle rock of the cradle, while voices within whisper a lullaby, restoring the mind from eternal toil to ephemeral rest.

CHAPTER ONE

In the heart of a seed,

Buried deep, oh, so deep

A dear little plant

Lay fast asleep

- 2nd Standard poem

Childhood memories are the sweetest.

The first awareness of my existence, and the very first visual memory: Climbing up the stairs, in the middle of the night, when four or five, to my parents' room on the first floor. Cuddling into the warm comfort of my mother's arms.

Going to bed when ten or twelve, mother drawing a light blue sheet over me, father smiling, switching off the light… figures receding into the darkness. Early days, warm and fresh in the mind's eye.

Stepping out of the cool aircraft two decades later on to Indian soil, my thoughts flutter from past to present, anchoring flashes that bring succour to a disenchanted mind. Savour it I must, before the magic wanes.

Memories of youth. Mixed flavour, at times bitter. Immigration, Customs… the counters flow past my physical frame. I have nothing to declare except my thoughts.

A clock at the airport lounge reads 2.55 a.m. A sleepy line of cabs await me as I step out of the terminal. The cab driver swings the meter flag, querying where I want to go… I struggle hard to pick a destination. A place to stay while I plan my escape from the prisons of the past.

1

I have wealth--plenty of it--and health, enough to propel my six-foot frame into long, solitary runs. If I could add a happy home – a wife plus a son or daughter – the picture would be complete. The loneliness from youth to middle age would never have enveloped my heart; memories trapped deep within would have given way to the present.

The truth is… the present has never held promise, because it only brings material comforts; the past has always held hope, because it continues to beckon, and if I try hard enough, some day I might return, to where I belong, ensconced in a world moving in reverse.

"Where you want to go sir?" The cabbie asks again, breaking my thoughts. I remember May Flower, to the left of Music Academy. A large, 3-star hotel where my father had treated me to truffle pudding. The flavour, and memories of my father, still linger fresh. "Go to Cathedral Road," I say confidently. "May Flower Hotel."

The cabbie gives me an "Are you from this century?" look. "Sir, May Flower closed; 20 years back, taking passengers there, driving taxi first time," he says in broken English, not knowing I speak Tamil. "When you come to Madras last?"

If there is a technique called astral travel, then I have visited this metropolis every day. No point telling the cabbie. He would drive me to Kilpauk, to the mental asylum. "Hmmmm. There was another hotel… name is…Chola," I say hesitantly, using fewer words to match his sparse English. "Near Music Academy… still there?

The cabbie brightens. Chola meant a well-heeled passenger I suppose. Ranked among the top three hotels at one time, still could be. As the cab exits the airport, I try to recollect its brick and mortar… inverted L-shaped car park, well-appointed lobby, coffee shop on the first floor, called Coorg or Mercara, furnished in a laid back style with sofas in checks of bright pink and light gray.

We exit the airport complex, turn left on the main road, and I realize that the airport itself is not the same. I mean it has moved, if such a thing can happen to airports.

"I say, what happened to the old airport?"

By now, the cabbie has got used to my ways. He lights a cigarette with both hands off the wheel, takes a deep drag, exhales, and remains silent for a few moments. Going back in time was not only my prerogative. "Thambi," he responds warmly, "This is new airport; old airport will come on left after two minutes, used now… only for sending cargo; I remember one time, I drop a passenger going to Bombay. Plane started from here, crashed."

* * *

The Caravelle was considered an advanced aircraft in 1979. It carried over 100 passengers, had the facility for night landing, and crashed only once in a while. As it taxied for take off, his mind replayed the farewell scene minutes earlier.

It was a late morning flight, on a Sunday. There were hardly 50 passengers and just a handful to see them off. In the halcyon days before hijacks and other threats, security was inconsequential. Visitors could enter at ease, and accompany kith and kin, almost to the fringe of the tarmac. His mother was there, proud and beaming, admiring her only son, and his travel clothes – neatly pressed white shirt, gray trousers, blue tie with subtle red stripes, and a blazer he carried nonchalantly on his arm. There were a few relatives to bid him farewell. Much to his surprise, she had come too. The second cousin with whom he had had his first brush with womankind, one otherwise serene Friday evening.

Were all women like her? Was she an exception? Did she overreact that day? He had never found out. In his journeys to the past, she was a frequent stopover. He knew he had done nothing wrong that Friday, but to be perceived as a potential wrongdoer hurt from deep within. Every time he was reminded of her, the heart would dole out an antidote to soothe the harsh memory: A drive-way lined with trees, a girl in distress, and a scented, pastel handkerchief that gave him reason to forgive the feminine gender.

As the aircraft took off and began its ascent, he peered through the window at his native city. He did not know when he would be back. The shutters of his mind opened to capture a spectacular top view of the sprawling, lush green polo grounds.

* * *

3

As the polo grounds flashed past on the left, dark and silent, I pressed the light button on my quartz watch. The menu was still set on chronograph, 2 hrs. 10 mins. I switched to time, date and the present.

Hotel Chola was unchanged. So was the doorman. I checked in, returned to the portico and signalled for the cabbie. He was chatting with a parking attendant. "How much should I pay for taxi from airport?" I asked the doorman. "Fare 150 rupees, night charge 75, tip extra if master wants."

As I paid up, adding a 30-rupee tip, I noticed the cabbie did not ask for more. Strange behaviour from a Madras taxi driver. "Thank you, Thambi," he said and moved on, content with the remuneration for an honest night's work. "I say, I have some rounds tomorrow… come in the morning at 9 no…" Come to Madras, and the local way of speaking English, embarking with 'I say' and ending a statement or question with "no," reverts naturally.

I unpacked quickly, ordered coffee and a serving of cookies. By 5 a.m., I was dressed in shorts, vest and shoes, all set for my daily routine - a brisk, long distance run. Today it would be down the memory lanes of Madras rather than the clean, winding roads of Boulder, Colorado.

Five minute warm up, body stretch, chrono set to 0, right turn at the gate, and I was off towards the coastline, rubber sole tapping its well-versed rhythm on tar, propelling me to Gandhi Statue and Marina Beach. Left turn at Queen Mary's College, easy pace towards Reserve Bank.

I knew this stretch of the beach well. The red tiled pavement, parallel to the shoreline, was lined with equidistant bronze statues of dark hue, erected about 400 feet apart, representing icons and characters from Tamil literature and history, such as Avvaiyar, crowned as the Tamil Grandmother, for her subtle wit. G.U. Pope, the European who came to Tamil country in early 17th century and learnt the language, ultimately writing couplets and poems as good as any by scions of the soil. His epitaph read, "Here lies a student of Tamil."

I remembered. The statues came up to commemorate the World Tamil Conference in the late 1960s. Triggered by the key word, "Tamil," my mind crept back in time, to annals of history swept into corners, absent in textbooks, and alive in just a few minds.

4

I reined in my thoughts, lest the reflections lead to oubliettes that I eschewed most, dislodging Trojans that taunt the psyche's quest for peace and harmony. Unwritten, forgotten chapters of the state's history, memories of my father who died young, and his killer whose eyes I wanted to look into.

Back to the present. The Royapettah High Road intersection at Bank of Madura. A workout of over 90 minutes, sweating sauna-like in what must have been 75 degrees Fahrenheit and almost 70% humidity. I wanted to stop, and warm down, but heart tugged at feet to proceed further, to Woodys, the stage of a curtain raiser in the drama of life. No reservations here. I could look back at will, and bask in the reminiscence of images bright and effervescent.

* * *

In the late 1970s, the drive-in restaurant on Cathedral Road was a 'happening' place.

True to its name, you could drive in, park in the open area close to the boundary wall, with only trees to eavesdrop on you, waiters dispassionate to your prolonged presence, and none to pressurize your exit. Here, you could partake of your favourite snack (never mind if you are part of the city's celebrity circuit). Or, you could stroll in on foot, or ride in on your two-wheeler, choose one of the two restaurants, and join the faithful with your plateful. The restaurants were split simply by an aisle - self service on the left, waiters on call on the right, and the old- world ambience spelt hospitality all around. The infrastructure included an air-conditioned dining room at the rear, and adjacent to the restaurants a shop selling cigarettes, toffee and peppermint.

The entire area, from the In gate and Out gate, each with its tree-lined driveway, and encompassing the car park, restaurants and children's play area was a few acres. Beyond the built-up and paved area lay unused land, full of brush, shrubs and undergrowth, stretching from the Cathedral Road tip opposite the American Consulate, and bound by a horseshoe-shaped compound wall, all the way up to Mount Road on the Teynampet side, adjoining the flyover.

Set up in the early 1960s when land was in abundance and lifestyle laid back, the drive-in spawned a generation of customers who came to unwind, meet friends or while away time. It was part of a chain of establishments belonging to a family from Karnataka. The idea of a drive-in restaurant was a novel experiment that succeeded, set as it was in an era that made no demands on time.

"Let's go to Woodys" was a familiar refrain among students, before and after an assortment of activities: college, Tamil film, English theatre, and that 70s trend christened "combined studies" that resulted in no study. Woodys was never considered a hot bed of romance, because boy and girl would be noticed too easily (Madras was then still a small town). Yet, it served as a starting point for many relationships, which would conveniently blossom elsewhere.

He came there often, mostly after college. He would greet a few known faces, order coffee, at times a dosa, and if he was feeling less melancholy and more cheerful, a plate of golden brown gulab jamun, the delectable dessert that struggles to stay afloat in sticky sugar syrup. He preferred the section served by Kasi Rao, the seniormost waiter at Woodys at that time.

The veteran knew his moods, and matching menu preferences. He could judge if the reticent visitor was ready to rifle the menu, or content mulling over a cup of coffee. At times, from the little shop inside, the young man would buy toffees, and retire to his favourite spot at the circular, concrete base of a huge tree just outside the restaurant area. Once a year, the tree would give vent to a charismatic tapestry of crimson-red flowers, each a curious gnome keen to know the twists and turns of the lives below.

The tree was a meeting point, hangout, and observatory rolled into one. It offered protection from elder brothers, fathers, uncles and aunts who were likely to drop in for tiffin (you averted such perils by finding a seat on the blind side of the ringed concrete base). As this was outside the restaurant area, there was no compulsion to order. Located at a tangent from the entrance, it offered a free view of every (female) visitor, without exposing your drool.

He did not know the name, or significance of the tree. A member of the Horticultural Society opposite Woodys would probably classify it as Flame of the Forest. Learned sages from the Vedic age might have added that the wood of the tree contained potential energy, which they could tap during yagnas. The inherent fire was otherwise released through its flaming orange flowers.

Partly by observing, partly from the small talk around the tree, he knew most of the student groups, and who was courting whom. He knew the relationships that would wither, and those that would last for a lifetime. As for himself, he had no expectations.

* * *

The greatest feeling in life is expectation. As the familiar sights came into view at half past six, 20 years later, my adrenaline rose, and pace quickened. Hotel Amaravathi, the TTK headquarters followed by Sanmar, Hotel Maris, Chola, Dr. Agarwal's eye clinic, the compound wall of Stella Maris and then Woodys. No one whom I knew would be there, at this early hour. The boys of the 70s who milled around the tree would have become men, the girls now mothers, the noisy Yezdi and majestic Enfield motorcycles would have given way to gleaming, purring Japanese two strokes, Premier Padmini to sleek European cars, and the past to the present.

About a 100 yards ahead of the drive-in gate, I stopped. My mission was just an hour old, and in many ways the drive-in was the destination, not the start point. For now, I would relish the recall, but not set foot inside the property. I turned around, locking the urge to step back in time, and set off at a smart pace towards Chola.

* * *

The lobby manager rang at 8.55 a.m., announcing the arrival of my taxi. I was emerging from a sumptuous South Indian breakfast spread: venn pongal for starters, dosa with sambar and authentic coconut chutney, a plate of rava kesari - the cream of wheat sweet dish made Madras style with loads of sugar, dollops of ghee and a lavish garnish of raisin, cashew and cardamom - washed down with heavenly filter coffee.

As I rode down in the plush elevator, I realised that like much of the hotel, this too had not changed. In a way, I had. Riding in the car 20 years earlier, I would have admired my reflection, checked out my shoulder width in the three-sided mirror as the elevator rode down. Over

7

time and with workouts, the blades had grown wider, but in my current mental state I was not inclined to narcissism.

As I neared the portico, I planned my day. I was carrying a parcel and a bag to hand over to parents of colleagues. The parcel was the usual almonds-saffron-chocolates routine which relatives of Non-Resident Indians ask for, the other some toys. I was in no mood for such visits and the inevitable small talk that would crop up about the absentee colleague and his spouse. "How are they? Can you come back before you leave? I want to send some badaam cake… and oh, you are not married? I know a good girl just right for you, she's only 32…" Best way out: write a note and ask the cabbie to drop off the stuff in the evening. Socializing is the norm for most people, yet such traits were non-resident in my persona.

* * *

The change from normal to unusual had been triggered by an untoward incident at an impressionable age. It happened one Friday evening, in his final year of college. He had come home as usual to spend a scheduled special hour with his mother. It was his habit to stand in a corner of the kitchen, left elbow atop the wooden larder. Sipping cocoa, he would share with her the day's events at college as she cooked the evening meal. She would chip in with family updates, and sundry news from the neighbourhood. An affectionate exchange that meant much to mother and son.

His father had died when he was just 14 years old, the year he had taken him to Hotel May Flower to savour a multi-layered truffle pudding. The boy still remembered the street lined with police jeeps and government vehicles, and a doorway strewn with boots, shoes and slippers, his mother staring at the body wrapped from head to toe in a white sheet, with no part of the face or flesh visible. The police hearse drawing away for the last journey. The hard-boiled men of the force wept like children when he lit the funeral pyre. No one deserved to be cremated twice.

Some of his melancholy could be attributed to his father's untimely death, some to his growing up as a single child, and the rest to the fear he had read in the girl's eyes that Friday evening. Was he untrustworthy? The question would haunt him all his life, causing him to shun the opposite sex.

8

On that fateful day, he had planned to visit the nearby playground for a round of "dips" on the parallel bars. He had a firm build like his father, and his daily routine served to strengthen his chest, shoulders and arms. He wore a light blue vest he had long outgrown.

Mother had innocuously asked him to carry a bunch of jasmine packed in a wet green leaf, tied with a strand of bark, to his aunt's house two streets away. A distant cousin from overseas, unaware of his mother's widowhood, had brought her the jasmine. His mother would normally have adorned the idols in the puja room with the flowers, but that evening she had not lit the lamp and offered prayers. After her husband's death, she had begun to doubt the existence of God, and only prayed on days when she felt so inclined. As a young man then, he had not realized why she had been in such a hurry to get the flowers out of the home, why their very presence troubled her like prickly heat.

Obeying his mother, the muscular young man, dreaming of non-stop dips on the parallel bars, picked up the flowers and absent-mindedly found his way to the aunt's house. All he planned to do was complete the chore and leave. His mind was elsewhere, and it was imperative to get his body there as well.

He pressed the doorbell but could not hear the customary shrill retort. He pressed again, to confirm its malfunctioning or the absence of electricity. He wondered if he should leave the flowers with the family who rented the first floor from his aunt. Going up and down would be a bother. He casually cranked the latch, and was not surprised when the door opened, for in the neighbourhoods of South Madras in the late 1970s, security was hardly a matter of concern. Doors would be shut, but not necessarily locked during the day.

He entered the hall, found no one. Ditto kitchen and dining room. Only the backyard and bedroom to the right of the hall remained to be explored. He was becoming impatient, for he would have to wait for his turn at the parallel bars.

Backyard first. Clothes drying on the line. A lone crow perched on the well. As he re-entered the kitchen, he heard the bedroom door open. His heart jumped. Time to be wary. A relative meekly waiting in the hall for an inhabitant to turn up would be accepted; if he was discovered moving freely around the home, his intent could be mistaken.

Like time in the cosmic clock, our actions cannot be reversed, and the young man, set to become a victim of youth and circumstance, reached the hall with uncertainty in every step.

The hall did not have sufficient natural light, and no lights were on either, indicating a power cut. The bedroom door was ajar, but from where he stood he could not see within. Had a female occupant just finished dressing, he wondered, and left the door open? The seconds ticked away, while he pondered his next step. Luck was still with him. He could gently step out and knock on the main door, retracing his steps. But if the occupant exited the room as he was leaving, explaining would become awkward. The other option was to knock on the bedroom door.

Inside the room could be aunt or cousin Nirupama, and very unlikely uncle. On further thought, he ruled out Nirupama, because she normally was away for music class at this time. Not to worry, he concluded, just open the door and say hello to aunt. Jasmine in hand, he took three further steps and reached the point where he could look inside.

No aunt, only Nirupama, fumbling with a pin that held her saree on to the blouse. He watched in fascination, as she carefully removed the pin - a silver brooch from what he could observe - dropped the top of the fabric down to her navel, and flung it back in a flourish. It apparently had not turned out right, for she dropped the saree top, pallu to be precise, a second time, admired her figure momentarily, and gathered it again. She pinned up now, satisfied with the drape. His vocal chords wanted to call out, but his nerves struck work, frozen by suppressed desires.

In the days gone by, when a premise could be said to mirror reality, it was held that a chicken moving on the ground would dart for cover when a hawk hovered high in the sky, but not when the bird was a harmless gull or heron. Among human beings, it is the weaker sex that nature endows more with such archetypal stimuli to sense an intruder.

The girl proceeded to set her hair, picking up two hairpins on the dressing table. She inserted one smartly in her mane, and placed the other between her teeth. At that moment, intuition caused her to turn around, capturing a mesmerized Arjun through the gap in the door.

He was no stranger to the house, yet his inappropriate presence put her off balance. Without moving a step or saying a word, she removed the hairpin and kept looking at him, eyes wide with fear and suspicion. Just then, the electricity came on, shedding light on his bulging shoulders, sinewy forearms, and the jasmine clutched in his palm.

"What are you doing here, Arjun? Is this is what you do, peep through the bedroom door?"

Given the privacy of the scene, and the chance intrusion, his honour had been questioned. Walking in was pardonable, moving around could be explained, playing voyeur could not be. His misdemeanour opened the door to a new destiny. It revealed to him an unknown world, one filled with suspicion, hate and fear, a dark universe where he was victim and quarry. She had seen him in a different light, and for the rest of his life, he could never clear the stigma.

"I am sorry Nirupama, I, I… I… did not mean any harm. The bell was not working, I just came in, and by mistake I saw you. Please understand," he said and reassuringly, and stepped into the bedroom, not realizing the remedy lay in keeping distance.

Neurosis is a trait embedded in every woman. More so in Tamil Brahmin women. Mothers teach them that chastity is the best bridal gift to their husband, and the thought of a breach can send them into a tizzy.

"Don't come near me. You knew Amma had gone for her club meeting. I know why you came!" she screamed, and raising her voice ever further, she called out hysterically to the young girl who lived in the first floor.

"Revathi, Revathi, come here fast, Arjun is troubling me!"

Truth arrives in various shapes, and at times in a lone sentence. He bent down, without taking his eyes off her, placed the jasmine on the floor as the flower vendor would do, turned and exited without saying a word.

He did not go to the playground for his workout that evening. Instead, he trudged around T' Nagar, frustrated and remorseful. His mind kept replaying the fear that had brimmed in Nirupama's eyes. He could picture the images her optical system transmitted to her brain: predator hunting for prey, and at worst, an outcaste in Brahmin garb.

While the devil plagued his mind, the gods were at work. His life was at the threshold of change, yet he knew not what lay ahead. The almost vacant house, the open door and tense woman within, were but preliminary manifestations of divine powers breaking into play. The jasmine was a destiny tool to place him in distress, the insult a divine decree to alter his outlook and spin his life in a new direction. He was about to be transported from his environment, from the warm cocoon of his protective mother and from the idyllic garden that signified youth. Ahead awaited the summons to a supreme event, the mythological Call to Adventure.

Unaware of fate tugging at the axis of his life, he boarded a bus to Woodys. Much like a child regaining its sense of control when read a familiar story, he was reaching his favourite haunt to regain balance. A chilled glass of lime juice inside the restaurant, and he returned to his usual seat below the flame of the forest, for his ringside view of humanity, from the concrete base of the tree, on one of the worst days of his youth.

Boy met girl.

* * *

CHAPTER TWO

"She is the paragon of all paragons of beauty,

the reply to all desire, the bliss-bestowing goal

of every hero's earthly and unearthly quest.

She is mother, sister, mistress, bride…

for she is the incarnation of the promise of perfection."

The narrator in Grimm's Fairy Tales describes the princess in the 'Frog Prince' story as one whom "the sun marvelled every time it shone on her face." The Indian sun is likely to vouch likewise for a certain girl who lived in Mylapore. If there was a differentiator between her and a thousand other women in South Madras, it was her subdued beauty.

She was an adolescent, discovering everyday the magic and mysteries of being one. Life was one constant cycle of college, chitchat, commuting and "combined studies," where the time spent in exchanging secrets most recently discovered would surpass the minutes spent on studies.

Living in the Mylapore-Mandaveli area as she did, her social outings were restricted to visits to the Kapaleeswarar Temple, wandering around the Madaveedhi market with friends, and snacking on banana chips and peanut balls at Ambi's Appalam Store.

To the uninitiated, this old style neighbourhood of Madras must be put into perspective: Mylapore stretches roughly from Luz Corner in the north to Mandaveli in the south, bounded by Santhome on the east and Abhiramapuram on the west. In many ways, Mylapore is representative of South Madras, known for its conservative attitude and austere living. The typical Mylapore girl studied at Lady Sivaswamy High School, the upper middle class at Rosary Matric, and others started out at Bon Secours Convent near Foreshore Estate.

To continue the typecasting, a typical upper middle class Mylaporean father would be a member of the Mylapore Club, shuffling cards at the spacious verandah, and the family would tuck into home-style 'tiffin' at its canteen. They would turn up in their Saturday best for film shows at the Club lawn. On Sundays, you would find them at Mylapore Fine Arts, taking in a play, concert or dance performance.

As to romance in those far off days, boys would woo girls with quick glances as they boarded Route No. 5 or No. 21, or during Friday evening darshan at Kapeeleswarar Temple. The girls would respond by turning their face away.

Dates were strictly restricted to the calendar. Girls who did fall in love would do so carefully, after ascertaining the boy's antecedents, family background and for added safety, his sub-sect.

As the 60s gave way to the 70s, the girls became bold. Iyers fell in love with Iyengars. They ventured out with boys, but in groups, or cliques, as they were known. Such outings were easy to explain at home. "Kamakshi's brother and two of his friends are coming with Jahnavi, Nitya, Vatsala and me for a movie…" that sort of a line worked with a parent puzzled by the changes in time. Despite such evolution, there were some, specifically mothers and a few young girls, who held steadfast to principles of the past, not necessarily from a platform of morality, but due to fear of the unknown. Which brings us to the Mylapore adolescent, the one marvelled at by the Indian sun.

* * *

She was the youngest of three daughters. Her sisters were 15 and 17 years older, for her birth was more an afterthought, caused by faulty reading of the father's horoscope, which indicated that a male offspring was in the offing. Nevertheless, the infant in the cradle, with eyes bright as a diamond and complexion akin to peach, seemed such a boon from heaven, the parents overcame the stigma that mandates a male child, and forgave the family astrologer. Being musically inclined, they named the little one after their favourite raga.

Her father believed she had brought him luck, for soon after her birth, he received a much overdue promotion, from DGM to GM, in the nationalised bank where he had started his career at age 21 as a Probationary Officer. Some nights he would wake up and switch on a soft light, and gaze at the toddler blissfully asleep in the roomy crib. He loved all his children, and unfair as it did sound, he loved the late arrival most. He wished the little angel would go through life without a hitch,

14

unaffected adversely by planetary movements, and spared the suffering of ordinary mortals.

Most of his prayers were answered. Within the top three ranks in Rosary Matric, distinction in the pre-university course, and effortless admission to B.A. English at Women's Christian College. Daddy's pet was no longer a little girl – he could observe the changes in her, physiological, emotional, intellectual, yet she always had a sense of balance that surprised and reassured him. He never preached to her on what was right and wrong. The protected environment she grew up in, the agraharam type of neighbourhood, and the non-invasive society of the times ensured her imbibing what he considered were requisite morals.

His wife was a silent influencer, imparting the right principles by signs and tokens, rather than sermons and warnings. The personality that emerged by the time she was in the second year of college was that of a well-bred young woman, introvert in the eyes of the male, shy in the eyes of her gender, and deep, to those who would have a chance to know her.

She was trained to hold back, to never express her emotions, especially with reference to the opposite sex. She would have the opportunity, figured her mother, for such outlets after marriage. Just two more years, her guard duty would be over, the virgin would be handed over intact. But times were changing, she would have to step up the vigil, monitor her circle of friends and her outings.

* * *

The young girl pulled out a lipstick from her handbag and turned the base. The snubbed, slightly pointed tip appeared in view. It was maroon in colour, contrasting her sunlit face. She applied a little, rubbed it out with the back of her palm, and applied again.

She wanted to go out with her friends; she did not want to. She wanted to meet the nice young men they said they had met yesterday. Last evening, she had had no intention of meeting them. She voted in favour in the night, vetoed next morning. And here she was at 5 p.m., dressed in her mother's chiffon saree, dabbling with cosmetics. Nice girls did not do things like that, her mother had always said. They went

15

to school and college, but never out with men. But come on, she said to herself, she was grown up, in her second year of college, and this was the late 70s, not the early 50s of her mother's youth. She was not really going out. She was going to a place where these young men would happen to be. She would say hello. If they said movie, party, let's go next Sunday to Silversands... of course she would not agree.

Once her sense of respectability was placated with reasoning, she had no further control over her actions. Her handbag moved from table to shoulder, her voice announced she was going out with friends, and soon she was in that hotbed of tasty food and happy youth, Woodys.

* * *

He spotted her the moment she neared the tree. None could enter the restaurant without crossing the area five feet from the concrete base. He knew she was new, from her extra casual look, and feigned air of confidence. She had to be from WCC, because her companions were from that clique. Probably B.A. English. He could have deduced more, but all he had was maybe 10 seconds as she approached the restaurant, and a few more before she turned left into the self-service area. While the observer in him was still active, he had no wish, after the afternoon incident, to interact with women: a paranoid gender that envisioned a rapist in every male.

A moment later he had forgotten her, because he had other issues on his mind. He blamed a series of events and people that had led to the jasmine episode. The death of his father, which had widowed his mother. The hooligan posing as a language activist, and the mob that spurred him.

A month after his father's death, he had visited the spot with a police officer investigating the gruesome crime. Being a good cop, he had turned up in plain clothes, put on a cap to hide his crew cut and posed as an insurance agent who was helping the boy receive his father's insurance benefits. They had talked to several people in the street, but most were reluctant to go into details. At a paan shop, they struck pay dirt.

In broken Tamil, the paanwala explained that a man had been seen rushing out of a large bungalow nearby, his face covered with a bright

Rajasthani veil and holding a burning piece of wood in his hand. In the home, they met an old lady and a 20-something Marwari youth. They claimed to have no knowledge of the man and rubbished the theory that the perpetrator had exited from their home. Apparently, during the agitation, they had shut the main doors when they saw activists entering their compound, looking for stones and other material to hurl at the policemen. "Do you have any servants in the house?" He remembered the officer asking the old lady. "We have two, one for sweeping and doing the dishes, one for cooking. They don't stay here but come and go."

"Where is the kitchen?" asked the inspector. "Outside the house, at the back, but inside the compound. This house was built 50 years ago, and in those days the kitchen was located outside. Only cooked food would be brought in."

"At the time of the riot, onlookers say that a man from your compound rushed out with a burning stick of wood, in Tamil we call it viragu…"

"No inspector, it is not possible. All the doors in our house were closed, and every window. The gate also was locked. Unless someone jumped over the gate inside the compound for their safety, and left after the riot."

"Do you have a car driver?'

"Er, well, we have a car, but never had a steady driver. They would leave because we don't have much work, and we do not pay high salary either. Maaf kijiye, here I am just talking to you without offering anything… can I make some tea for you people?"

They prowled the street for more clues but had no further luck. Over time, like many other acts of arson, looting and murder that go unsolved in violent protests, this investigation too came to a slow halt. The file was closed after a few years. But not in his mind. The street, the paanwala and for some reason the Marwari lady, rather something she had said but not fully revealed, flitted in and out, especially when he was upset with something else.

Perched in his ringside seat, reliving the anguish of the past, he detected a warm glow from the present. It could not have been the afternoon, it would have to be something he had observed right here. Ah, the slender woman from WCC... dressed in chiffon, blessed with the skin tone of peach. He needed a distraction, to take his mind off Nirupama. He decided he would watch the slender girl from a safe distance. He reached the shop and bought some toffees, unwrapping two and glancing casually at her group.

* * *

She is seated in a ring of seven, four boys and three girls. Quiet, withdrawn and apparently nervous. The boy to her right leans towards her and says something softly. She turns away. The boy says something to her again. He recalls the boy's name as Sudhakar, an arrogant sort from an abrasive group.

Next to him is a boy named Rocky, a college dropout whose trick is to befriend students, get them hooked to ganja, and then peddle the stuff he procures from hippies in Mahabalipuram.

Sensing trouble, he troops in, and takes a chair at the next table.

"Oh, look at your hand, it's become red. Did you hurt yourself? Here, let me see," Sudhakar says, touching the back of the girl's palm where there is a red swish.

"Don't touch me," she snaps in a low voice, not wanting to draw attention.

"So you are the hard-to-get type, is it?" Sudhakar holds her hand again.

The girl is bewildered. She cannot figure out what her reaction should be. Having accepted to share a table with these boys she has signalled her willingness to mix with the opposite sex. Reality was far apart from Mills & Boon. The handsome hero, a far cry from this overbearing brute with hair in his forearms and a sneer on his face. Minus that expression he is not bad looking... probably a spoilt brat from a rich family... not the best time for analysis, for he is holding her wrist firmly.

"Leave me alone, please, I have met you for the first time, and I don't think you should be behaving like this," she says with a firmness that surprises Sudhakar. Yet, his ego does not permit him to withdraw.

18

"I will let go, only if you promise to come with me for a drive. Come sweetheart, we are wasting time here, let's take a spin up to Marina beach, and tomorrow let's go to Mahabs." He rises, still holding her by the arm.

"Machi, take a room at Silversands, spend the day with her, and give her what she wants... you know what I mean," Rocky egging on Sudhakar. "Sudhakar, please, stop it," one of the boys pleading weakly.

"She is a Mylapore girl. Let her go."

"I love girls from Mylapore da. They are fresh and full of surprises."

"I am from Mambalam," declares a stern voice from behind. Hands of steel clamp on Sudhakar's shoulders, causing him to drop the girl's hand and spin around.

A wiry young man, about six feet tall, with chiselled biceps and sinewy forearms. Lost look in his eyes, yet in sufficient focus to handle the situation.

"Who are you, her boyfriend or uncle?" Sudhakar asks with all the sarcasm he can muster. "We are all friends here, and we're just playing around, ok, so why don't you mind your business?" he adds, jabbing at the young man's chest, causing him to step backward.

For a moment, the saviour is nonplussed. "Miss, tell me all is well, I will leave."

The girl responds with silence and an examination of her toes. "See, she is quiet, that means yes," Sudhakar says, forcing the young man to go on the back foot again. "Just get out of here, you roadside Romeo!"

Embedded in each of us is a sense of justice, an inner desire to ensure that right is not perceived as wrong. As Sudhakar heaped insult on the young man, the girl who had stepped out of her protected world into the world of a protector, decides that truth would not be a casualty in the episode.

"I don't know who you are, but I would like to thank you for intervening... I am leaving," she says to her friends. "You people stay."

"Let me take you home. Come with me." It surprises him to hear his own voice, even more when she nods in acceptance. He escorts her out of the restaurant, past the Flame of the Forest, the driveway with its avenue of trees, out of the verdant compound, to the Out Gate. More than being beaten to pulp, this is the worst sentence Sudhakar could receive, and more than saying thanks, trusting a stranger's company is a superlative acknowledgement of her gratitude.

Crossing the road with the girl in tow, he feels a sense of elation. Life has changed in a flash. From being the knave that afternoon in an overwrought woman's imagination, he has metamorphosed by evening into a valiant knight. There is someone at work, balancing a minus with a plus.

A Yezdi motorbike in low gear and engine in high rpm emerges from the Out gate, the rider checks cursorily for oncoming cars in the failing evening light and darts across the road, braking to a halt a foot away from him. The girl recoils as she recognizes Rocky in the saddle. Henchman to avenge insult. In one quick motion, Rocky parks using the side stand and without a warning or war cry lunges at her saviour. He steps aside smartly. Rocky gropes below his waist and unbuckles a metal chain worn like a belt and swings it at the young man, who ducks in quick reflex, but the last link nicks the left earlobe. The masochist does not flinch.

"Don't' fight him, Rocky. He is very strong, and if anything happens all of us are in trouble," a boy in the group who has cycled down to the exit, screams from the other side.

Rocky hesitates. The boy on the other side of the road calls out again. Just then an auto rickshaw, unaware of the proceedings and presuming the couple is awaiting a ride, pulls up. Rocky backs off at the presence of a third party.

They quickly board the auto and she instructs the driver to take them to Mandaveli. His earlobe stings, but he chooses to ignore the pain. As the three-wheeler passes Music Academy and nears Savera, her self-control dissipates and she breaks into tears.

"I have never come out with boys. I thought they would be such nice people. This was the first time. I will never do this again." She opens her handbag, fumbles, and draws out a pastel kerchief with an embroidered monogram, even as he hesitantly pulls out his. If he could actually dab at her cheeks, wipe the tears… and comfort her. In her present state, she might misinterpret his compassion. Yet, with her forlorn face and teary eyes, she suddenly looks so vulnerable, he wants to hold her in his arms and guard her forever.

His mind reviews the girl's predicament. Probably from a conservative family. No talking to boys except friends of her brother if she had one. He imagines her room, a study desk at one corner, wooden almirah for clothes, single bed, and pin ups of film icons from North and South – most likely Kumar Gaurav and Kamalahasan, along with Sridevi and Vidya Sinha.

She huddles in the bench seat, eyes closed. In the narrow confine, the drape of her saree extends from her slender shoulders on to the seat, and he finds a portion of the drape, silky soft chiffon, resting on his shoulder. The ache intensifies, but he decides against drawing attention to the injury. No room for the trivial in an instance so precious.

He wants to prolong the vicarious touch, suspend time and stay connected, but like many of life's precious moments this too has to pass. They cross Shanti Vihar on the left and Mylapore Pharmacy on the right, and reach Luz corner en route to Mandaveli. If she lives on the Santhome border, they would have to turn left on Kutcheri Road and approach Mandaveli via Rosary Matric. "Listen, which way do we go, left, or straight?"

She does not answer. He repeats the question twice before realizing she is not receptive to sound, probably a reflex reaction to the intrusion of privacy, or a self-induced coma to shut out the big, bad world. He draws his palm reluctantly from beneath the drape, rolls his handkerchief into a ball and taps her shoulder, ensuring his fingers do not touch her smooth flesh. She does not respond. Concerned, he taps her again with his kerchief. She wakes with a start. She says she lives in Trustpakkam, and with that necessary disclosure, lapses into silence.

The three wheeler trundles further, past the Mylapore Tank, Ramakrishna Mutt and PS High School, bearing a boy and girl who have met by chance the for first time in their 19 odd years. He has not asked her her name; and if she has to know his, he must volunteer it. He concludes that such stimuli, or the lack of them, are an attribute of her personality, shaped by safeguards advocated and honed by her sterile environment.

Trustpakkam is a set of three streets, off Mandaveli Market Road and perpendicular to a street that houses a little known hotel called Admiralty. He guides the auto in the failing evening light along the market road. He senses she would not want to be dropped off at home for two reasons: A neighbour might notice them, giving rise to gossip, or a parent would ask questions. And she might fear that he would return another day with relationship-building questions such as "How are you feeling now? Is everything all right?"

"When we near your street, tell me. I will get down. You can take the auto home," he offers chivalrously. He is not surprised when she hems and haws but finally agrees.

He knows she just wants to forget the sudden turn of events, and return to her secure world of parents and pin ups, away from people adverse, alien and oppressive to her gentle, trusting nature. In a way, she is a mirror image of his personality, misunderstood and persecuted by the opposite gender.

The auto halts at Admiralty. The girl is blissfully unaware of the profound impression she has made on him. Her dominating concern is arriving home without the family knowing something is amiss. She delves into her hand bag, pulls out a long comb, quickly unfastens the clip holding her hair, places the clip between her teeth, shakes her tresses loose, and brushes her hair with long, sweeping strokes. The young man watches spellbound. Next she adjusts the pallu of her saree, and wraps the loose end around her shoulders. Her expression changes as her fingers find it sticky, and she looks at him anxiously.

Blood. Dripping from his earlobe on his neck and her saree when the drape has unwittingly fallen on his shoulder.

"Don't worry about me, the tip of the chain hit my ear. The bleeding will stop in a while," he says casually. She hunts for her handkerchief in her handbag but it's missing. Words cannot remedy physical hurt. With the edge of the pallu, she carefully cleans the blood on his neck, exploring by touch for further wounds. Her warm finger rests for a fraction longer on his blood. Time for him to get down; chances of passersby recognizing her are high.

"Please, please see a doctor on your way home," she says as he leaves. He accepts her thank you, notes her relief at his appropriate exit from the scene.

He does not walk back to the market road, but remains standing outside the hotel. He knows the side street well, knows it is a dead end. Most parts of South Madras are mapped in his mind. The auto would have to drop her home and return the same way, and he could hail it again. Hearing no sound for almost a minute, he enters the street with cautious steps. He sees her again, coming out from a small, independent house; you could hardly call it a bungalow because it had no frills or design, just a flat home without even a first floor. She must have gone in to bring change. Sometimes, auto rickshaw drivers would deny having any, in the hope of pocketing the balance.

She returns home, the three-wheeler makes a U-turn, and he boards it near the hotel. As they pass a streetlight, he finds her pastel handkerchief on the floorboard, damp with her tears.

* * *

"Sir, your taxi, sir... master's taxi waiting sir," the doorman was saying. I fought my way back to the present. It was hard to believe that two decades had passed. I would have to look ahead, not dwell in the past, in order to complete my mission.

In 10 minutes, we were at Mandaveli market. The place had not changed much. I was able to guide the cabbie to the street where I had waited for the auto to return. Admiralty Hotel was no longer in existence. It had been converted as the staff quarters of a nationalized bank. I alighted and stood outside the same gate, 20 years later, wondering what other changes in brick and mortar, and in people and places had taken place. Finding the dead end street was easy. I knew her house was the third on the right. I would ask for her, but did not expect her to be around. She would have married by now, become a mother and a devoted wife to a fortunate husband.

My only fear was the house, along with the adjoining plots, might have been converted into an apartment complex. This would make enquiries more complicated.

The house was still there, but looked better. The bare land around was now rich green, with creepers, flowerpots and a patch of lawn on one side. The name board proclaimed Lt. Col Sukumaran (Retd.) – Corps of Engineers. A sprightly old man, in shorts and T-shirt, carrying a dumbbell in one arm, answered the bell. I couldn't figure out if the weight was for protection, or if he was merrily exercising at 10.30 in the morning.

"Sir, I knew a family that lived here 20 years ago. There was a girl here studying in Women's Christian College. Do you know where to the family has moved?"

"You must be looking for my tenants. They left this house long, long ago, some 15-16 years back. I don't know where they are now." He proceeded to close the door without further ado.

"Colonel, I am sorry I disturbed you. Tell me, is that a 10-pounder? It's good for building up muscle tone, as long as you do high reps per set."

Talk to health freaks, in the language they understand, and they will mellow. The man's face lit up. "I have heavier weights too. But the doctor has told me to go easy. Why don't you come in?"?

It turned out Colonel Sukumaran had moved back to his home soon after retirement. He showed me his collection of chrome-plated weights, all gleaming with daily care. I told him that my father had been in police service, and the disclosure established instant rapport. He asked about my life in the US, to which I responded briefly. I asked him about his tenants again in my best casual manner.

"You must know the third daughter. The other two don't live in Madras any more. If I remember, one is in Trichy, and the other in Coonoor." He said the third daughter had written to him last about 12 years ago to say that her parents were no more. The mother had died of cancer, and the father of heart failure a month later.

"The daughter who wrote to you... I knew her well at one time, but lost touch," I said with all the confidence I could feign. "Is she married too?"

The old codger looked me straight in the eye, sensing the import of the question.

"Yes, my boy, she is jolly well married. I still have the wedding invite, and her last letter. Why, I preserve just about everything. I will give you her address."

He copied the address from the diary on to a slip of paper. I noticed he did not write the girl's name on it. If I asked him her name, I would fail the test, and stand exposed.

"Well, thanks Colonel. I must get going," I said as I collected the address. "You take care and take it easy."

Married? She had to be. Whom would she have married, I speculated, as the taxi wound its way past the familiar sights and surroundings of Mylapore. A distant relative, family friend or a perfect stranger whose horoscope matched with hers? Did the man know how lucky he had been, to walk into the life of one of the most beautiful women on earth, an angel in human form? Had she, for a millisecond, compared the boy who helped her that evening, with her husband?

The complexities in my mind and the confirmation of her marital status in no way diminished my urge to find her. Plodding on with the only clue I had, I approached the multi storeyed apartment, her last known address given to me by Col. Sukumaran, and drew a blank.

Apparently, the girl and her family had moved out many years ago. The present inhabitants had no clue to their whereabouts. The setback did not put me off. Hardly. I decided to assign the search to a professional, a deputy superintendent of police, Korattur Kumaravel. While the decision was logical, it took some amount of self-persuasion to actually take the step. Not that I doubted the inspector's investigative abilities. Assigning the task would mean meeting him, and stirring up old memories. I relished revisiting my mother's past, but my father's was a different story, thanks to his violent end. .

* * *

Inspector Kumaravel was an intellectual rather than a policeman. He had the air of a professor on sabbatical, impatient to return to his academic fiefdom. He was of slight build, wore a loose a fitting tunic, smoked two packs of cigarettes a day, held a master's degree in sociology, and had enrolled for M. Phil. at the University of Madras.

Three years after he joined the service, and after surviving riots, encounters and skirmishes, he wrote a long letter to the Director General of Police, requesting for a transfer to the Criminal Investigation Department. A battery of tests and a round of interviews proved what he already knew: that he had an intuitive, inquisitive mind. He could change his point of view 180 degrees and map the process of a crime, as carried out by the criminal. He could deduce the socio-economic factors behind the motive, which would often lead to the trail. His investigation reports would address the Why, not just the How. He advocated, with little success, a proactive role for the police, wherein it would help change society, rather than merely upholding the law. In many ways, he was a misfit, yet a much respected one.

I found him at the police HQ, deep in thought, behind a cluttered, expansive desk and below an ancient, slow-moving fan. He came around the desk on seeing me, and ignoring my held out hand, embraced me in a warm hug. I brought him up to date, sure his well trained mind was building a mental picture of my career overseas, and my unstated bachelor status. His eyes widened just a little as I briefed him about a girl I knew years ago, and wished to reconnect with for old times' sake. As I filled him with the details, his professional interest overtook his curiosity. Trust a good cop to yearn for a tough chase.

The business part over, the talk turned to family, and inevitably to my father, and his colleagues. I enquired about the inspectors whose wives would visit home when we had the "kolu" display during Navaratri. I asked after his family, and as he was responding, a bell rang somewhere within my mind, bringing forth the image of my father's Willys Jeep, the crackling of wireless, and the impassive constable who drove it – Mathivanan. I made a mental note to take his address before I left.

"Uncle, I know it's been 30 years, but I will ask this question all my life… Any update on the case? Are you close to finding my father's killer?"

"The file has been closed, Arjun, for over two decades now. We did get more clues. But there were hurdles to the investigation. The many transfers meant inadequate follow up. The FIR remains a case against unknown persons."

"The language issue, is it still an issue today?"

"No longer, I would say. People have realized that languages have to coexist. We do not live in compartments anymore. There is so much migration from one state to another that the more languages we speak the better."

"Had there been enough effort then, by the Government and the agitators to understand the issue–the reason for imposing a language and the resistance to accepting it– there would not have been so much bloodshed. Protestors, police, CRPF, so many valuable lives were lost."

"But uncle, why? What gave rise to the agitation? Was it negative feeling against the language that led to so much death and destruction?"

The learned policeman glanced at me keenly. He placed his palm downward on his desktop bell, causing it to emit a shrill sound, the signal for his peon to come inside. "Ah, Palani, two cups of strong coffee, and get me some cigarettes.

"Well, Arjun," he began presently, leaning back on his chair, stretching his long legs below the desk, and taking a sip of the chocolate brown canteen coffee. "I don't have a one-line answer to your question. Strangely, this subject, anti-Hindi agitation,, was never reviewed by the government or by sociologists. Not many documents are available in the files. There was no inquiry commission set up to probe the deaths on either side. To satisfy my personal curiosity, I did quite a bit of research.

"Buddhist monks in Vietnam immolated themselves to protest against religious persecution. Americans resorted to immolation to protest against the Vietnam War. Our own freedom fighters engaged in fasts unto death to expel the British. But when the juggernaut started rolling in Tamil Nadu, it was perhaps the first time in the world that language fired such fatal passions.

"Indian history has no trace of these events, and you will find sparse mention in the State records too. It is an issue not many remember, while people like you whose lives have changed course, can never forget it. Let me go back in time and recap the anti-Hindi agitation and its causes. Where shall I begin?"

* * *

CHAPTER THREE

The world as we know it, as we have seen it, yields but one ending:

death, disintegration, dismemberment, and the crucifixion of our heart

with the passing of the forms that we have loved.

Circa 1964. The early rays of the sun crept on the State of Tamil Nadu, bringing light that would shine on nooks and corners, people and places, history and horror. As the mercury rose with the rising sun, one man was rising to a cause, in the city of Tiruchirapalli, His name: K. Chinnasami. Occupation: Shop owner. Passion: Tamil.

Chinnasami stepped out of his modest abode and set off towards the main road. He reached the city railway station, his chosen destination to demonstrate his unswerving commitment. Swiftly, he doused himself from head to toe with kerosene, and stoically struck a match, going up in flames and down in history, as an activist who laid down his life in the anti-Hindi agitation.

It was a protest movement that had its seeds sown during British rule. As early as 1938, the Government of the Madras Presidency decreed that Hindi would be a compulsory subject in schools, which sparked protests and led to arrests. The anti-Hindi sentiment continued over the next 25 years, triggered by frequent proposals from the Central Government to impose Hindi in Tamil Nadu.

The landmark year was 1950, the year of the framing of the new Indian Constitution. From 26th January that year, Hindi was made the official language of India. The framers envisaged the implementation of Hindi as the sole official language, exactly 15 years later, on 26 January 1965. During the interim period, English would also serve as an official language.

Anti-Hindi protests reached a crescendo in 1963, but it took two eventful years for the imposition to meet its Waterloo. College students and members of political parties held black flag demonstrations and rallies, smeared tar on Hindi name boards in Central Government offices, and even burnt copies of the Indian Constitution.

The Army, Central Reserve Police Force and police forces from other States were brought in to quell the protests. According to unconfirmed reports, over 500 protestors fell to the bullets of law enforcement agencies or were killed during riots and protests. Peace returned in 1965 only when the Indian Government agreed not to impose Hindi in Tamil Nadu.

While the sacrifice made by those who fought to protect their native language is noteworthy and commendable, its dark and ugly side cannot be ignored. Taking advantage of the protests, several hooligans, not connected to the cause but bent on plunder, indulged in arson, and looting. And among the protestors fighting for a cause, there were outlaws who committed vile acts that set off anarchy and mayhem – the gruesome burning, not of property, parchments or books, not the symbolic combustion of a man-like, lifeless bogey, but of policemen in flesh and blood.

* * *

Kumbakonam Krishnan Kumaramangalam. The schoolmaster carefully copied the name from the Birth Certificate and studied closely the boy who faced him. He had his own inhibitions and his own theory on long names. It was a forewarning to an antithesis – the brevity of the person's life span.

His children had just a short name preceded by a single initial. Should he suggest "K.K. Krishnan"? It was none of his business really, plus the man accompanying the child was a policeman who would not put up with any monkey business.

"What is your father's name?" he asked officiously. He knew it was not Kumbakonam that being the town name, it was not Krishnan because that was probably the boy's given name, but then when you teach in school, you have the liberty to ask obvious questions.

"Kumaramangalam, sir", the boy responded smartly, unconsciously moving closer to the towering figure dressed in khaki tunic and 'policeman's' shorts, characterized by its loose fit and starched cotton fabric.

The boy wrapped his right arm around the man's right leg, pressing his face on to a thigh that closely resembled a rock, silently proclaiming the presence of his big, strong father. It was a small gesture, but an innocent one that can melt even the strong hearted. The father stooped, picked up the child in one easy motion and hugged him close.

"Chinna paiya, going to school, are you? Study well, and never fear!" For the little one, a valuable moral conveyed in childhood, and treasured for a lifetime. On this warm note commenced the boy's academia. He would leave home at 9 a.m. every day from his home in Mettu Veedhi, Kumbakonam, armed with a schoolbag laden with books and lunch. Right or wrong, he had a limited interest in studies all through school. Not that he was dumb or indifferent, but sometime in the eighth form, young Krishnan realized what his station in life would be, and set himself goals that would help him arrive. He was intelligent, and cleared his exams without fuss. He focused his energy on his physique, and chose sports that he hoped would make him taller, broader and stronger. From his earliest lucent memory of his father dressed in khaki, he had known always what he wanted to become: a just and upright policeman.

He learnt to swim in the town tank faster than his peers, and swam faster than his peers. He trained to hold his breath underwater longer than others. He played every kind of sport available to a young lad in Kumbakonam in the early 1940s. Kabaddi (he was a dreaded invader who could chant kabaddi, kabaddi, kabaddi, with a miraculous supply of oxygen, a powerful defender who could pin the enemy down till his breath ran out), Silambattam (his speed with the swirling stick soon became local legend, and only his master could take him on, but not for long), cricket (he tried, but soon gave it up, not because he couldn't make a mark, but because he preferred to burn energy rapidly within an hour, rather than expend it over half a day), running (oh, what a way to push the body! he had said to himself on his maiden attempt to run to his ancestral village miles away). Long distance running as a sport was unknown in Kumbakonam in those early days, but the small town lad loaded with native intelligence soon discovered that the activity added higher energy burn if enriched with obstacles en route. So he ran cross-country, jumping over hedges, fences and pumpsets, across rice fields, mangroves and brick kilns, along country roads and village lanes, getting fitter and faster by the day.

When he finished his Intermediate, he walked straight from the exam hall to the local gymnasium. From there on, it was a happy world of bench presses, wrist curls, snatch and jerk, and sit-ups. After completing a bachelor's degree in History, he turned up for selection at the police grounds in Tanjore, looking exactly like what he had set out to be: a tough as nails police officer.

For the selection trials, he had to choose six events out of nine and excel in the chosen ones. He chose high jump, long jump, rope climbing, wall climbing, running and swimming, leaving out cricket ball throw, shooting and pole vault. Next, a written test based on his graduate discipline, followed by an interview. He was selected and posted at the Police Training College, inside Vellore Fort along with 59 other batch mates. Early morning PT, followed by a gruelling parade. Classes through the day imparting relevant sections of the IPC, CRPC, Indian Evidence Act and local laws. Games and library hour in the evening. Roll call for 60 tired trainees at 9 pm. He emerged a year later as a Sub Inspector with two stars on his tunic, on a princely pay of Rs. 250 a month. A lifelong wish fulfilled.

His first posting was in Salem district, and he was promoted and transferred three years later to Madras. Bachelor life at the police quarters, dining in the police mess. Made in charge of the passing out parade, he placed an order for "sweet, savoury and coffee" with a caterer. With the Chief Minister expected to grace the function, he visited to the catering establishment in West Mambalam to ensure quality and timely delivery. Not a soul in the hall. Only a cook in the kitchen, receiving him with fear and respect. Directing him to the terrace.

Appalam, vattal, and salted lime drying in the hot sun. Caterer's niece, crouched under an umbrella, Deepavali Malar magazine in hand, lost look in her eyes. Rising on seeing the imposing visitor, speaking to him with downcast eyes, confirming the order, and that their team will arrive well ahead of time. Cloth patch on the blouse, worn out half saree, eyes that seek a future when there is none. Vulnerable, very vulnerable. She is protecting edibles from the birds. He wants to protect her for life. Asking him to have a cup of coffee before leaving. Climbing down the stairs. He tries not to look at the soft skin of her back, tries to block the scent of shikakai stemming from her hair, but too late, she is already in his heart. Her fingers touch his as he takes the coffee tumbler. Eyes

31

meet, his mind decides. In this life and the next, Marakatham will be his wife.

Birth of a son, four years later. If Marakatham was joy, the son is sheer delight. Happiness at home, satisfaction at work. Wheeling the son around in a tricycle at home. Taking the family around in his police Bullet, to Jaffar's Ice Cream near Elphinstone (Marakatham mistakes the wafers perched on top of the peach melba to be the spoon to eat the ice cream), to the newly-opened Woodlands Drive In Restaurant near Gemini studio (Marakatham is puzzled how people could eat in a car, he explains such practices could become popular in the future. A waiter who has just joined that day, Kasi Rao is his name, concurs with the view, and playfully gives the child a pinch). To a Tamil play at Krishna Gana Sabha (directed by a debutant named K. Balachander, a refreshing play, but Krishnan wonders whether the audience is mature enough to appreciate such treatment), each day, each place, adding another brick to his treasurehouse of memories.

Their life and its gentle rhythm are about to change, as winds of change blow across the nation. Year 1963. Official Languages Bill introduced in Parliament. Tamil leaders oppose the Bill. The imposition of Hindi opposed in Tamil Nadu. Police firing, protests, more police firing, more protests. A deathly cycle that wrings out peace and harmony.

The State's Home Minister handpicks a crisis management team from the police force, Inspector Kumaramangalam is proud to be part of it, but unaware that the appointment is about to shortcircuit his lifespan. The team reviews every facet of the problem and works on solutions as well – political causes, sociological reasons, riot control measures, formation of peace committees with multi-language representation, relief for riot victims...

The Director General of Police, a learned man who believes the baton is not the only answer to the question of how to curb the problem, invites a sociologist to address the crisis management team.

"Gentlemen," begins Dr. Siddharth Ghosh, the Stanford-trained professor, addressing the group at the police headquarters, a heritage building opposite the Gandhi statue, alongside Marina Beach, Madras. The 22 members of the crisis team expect no enlightenment from the professor. They look at him condescendingly, as though to say, 'You go back to your class, we'll go back to the field, where we belong.'

"Gentlemen of the police force, I am aware I am addressing the toughest band of officers in your State police. But battles are not won by rifles alone. Crowds are not controlled by just tear gas. Before you lead your men in the field, I want you to understand the conflict you have set out to control. For the first time in Indian history, the conflict does not stem from religion, caste or community, or from usurping of land by the enemy. The root cause is what people of your home state believe is the imposition of an alien language, Hindi, to be precise. Let me give you a quick lesson in history...

"It was in 1949 that the concept of a national language was first thrown open to debate, at the Constituent Assembly, to be precise. At that time, it was claimed by proponents of Hindi that the language was understood by 140 million people among a national population of 330 million. In contrast, the moderate view was that imposition of Hindi on such a rationale would actually lead to disintegration of the nation, and therefore the moderates offered English as an alternative. Ultimately, Hindi was declared the national language. When the Official Languages Bill was introduced recently in Parliament, your esteemed leader, C.N. Annadurai, pointed out that while 42 per cent Indians understood Hindi, this 42 per cent comprised people from the North.

"I trust the socio-political backdrop to the protests is clear. Today, you are gathered here to chalk out a crisis management plan, to control the rioting and arson that is breaking out in different parts of the State. The key to the riot control is an understanding of psychology of the rioter who rides on the platform of language to justify his unlawful acts.

"The common man, the typical officegoer or businessman, the taxi driver or shopkeeper, does not indulge in, or take part in a riot. Even if they are part of a procession, they may not be part of the violence that may erupt. Violence is the domain of certain seasoned professionals who are otherwise criminals in their own right, indulging in robbery, murder and extortion in their territory. To these professionals, a riot situation offers what we sociologists call a 'moral high.' Wearing the shroud of saviors of an oppressed community, these seasoned professionals indulge in vile acts that benefit vested interests. I hope I am making sense."

33

"What really is the best way to dissuade the rioter from rioting?" asks the DGP.

"Just remember that rioters are not like the kamikaze from Japan. They will not riot at the risk of losing their lives. So the best advice I can give you is, increase the personal risk of the rioter. If he sees a massive deployment of police or troops, if he finds they are armed to the teeth and authorized to shoot to kill, then his sense of bravado and self-induced moral high will wither."

The DGP signals for attention, realizing this is a critical moment to convey a key message to his men. "Officers, I ask you while doing your duty to watch out for professional rioters. Spare the general public but do not spare these criminals. They may act like soldiers, but they are just goondas, just shoot them on sight.

"Professor, I have a question." As Kumaramangalam speaks, all eyes turn on him.

"Even when we kill a person in the line of duty, the feeling of guilt at taking a human life stays with us for a lifetime. The man we have shot may be a criminal, but we know he leaves behind dependents, his wife, and children. How can these goondas who destroy public property, and take another's life, carry on with life?"

"I will answer that," the learned professor responds warmly, appreciating the depth of the question. "Such an extremist may be right next to you tomorrow when you are walking on the street, just another person in your neighbourhood. What happens is - during the agitation, the enemy is viewed as a demon. In this case, the demon is the Hindi language, and you as police officers are seen protecting the demon, while in truth you are protecting the public, and public property. You as the protector of Hindi, their enemy, become dehumanised, subhuman, and though you speak the same language as the rioter, you are identified with the enemy, so they have no qualms about attacking you or taking your life.

"The irony is that the goonda identifies his acts during a riot as acts of war. His strong, paranoid emotions at the time give way to his normal human emotions after the event, and he switches back to his personal identity. He can live normally for years afterwards. At least from the outside, he will appear normal."

Just then the DGP's aide rushes into the room. "Sorry sir, to butt in like this. The police station at Sowcarpet in North Madras is surrounded by language activists. They have radioed for help."

The DGP turns to his team: "Men, it is time to put into practice what Professor Ghosh has told you. Kumaramangalam, you know the area well, you take charge. Lead the convoy to Sowcarpet. And remember, put the rioter at risk."

* * *

Kumaramangalam in the lead jeep. Police driver on his right. Four seasoned policemen in the rear. Three vans carrying armed police close behind. Sirens wailing like a banshee through the streets. Convoy speeding towards Sowcarpet. Madras in the grip of language agitation.

Kumaramangalam flipped the button off his revolver holster, removed the weapon and cradled it in his palm. Somehow, something told him this was not just another mission. If handled right, it could be the turning point – maybe a promotion, an increment, maybe better quality work as in the crime branch, more time to spend with Marakatham and young Arjun.

Like many men with a harsh exterior, Kumaramangalam had a soft interior. He liked spending time with his family, but would never voice such a liking. He liked his wife's docile attitude. He sensed there was a sense of purpose in her life, and knew it had a finite scope. He knew her specific goal too - to be by his side forever. It was her way of expressing gratitude for his marrying a poor girl from a humble family. Her gratitude had become two-fold, when he fathered a son.

The birth of Arjun had changed his life too. Until then, he had always been clear about the import of his life as a policeman: on one side steady growth and the other, sudden death. Now the reality, rather the possible dawn of reality, troubled him. He wanted to be around to watch his son grow up. He wanted to be with his wife, as she grew old. He would want her to go first; he could possibly live without her. He was sure she could not survive without him.

He had enjoyed the outing last week to Jaffar's Ice Cream Parlour. Arjun had been thrilled while riding on the Bullet's fuel tank.

Marakatham was the pillion rider and the 350 cc Royal Enfield machine had carried them around town, chugging like a train engine. They had stopped for tiffin at the Woodlands drive-in. The family had stood for a few minutes at the base of a huge tree, blossoming with bright red flowers, and admired the scene. Waiters carrying trays of food and water, people either seated in cars or lounging in the restaurant with a cup of coffee. As they had left for home, well fed and refreshed, he knew he was the world's happiest man.

While his thoughts strayed, his ear was tuned to riot updates crackling from the wireless. A protest rally in Sowcarpet, home to the Hindi-speaking Marwari community, a place where nameboards were more likely to read Kishore Sonthalia and Dhiraj Gupta rather than K. Subramaniam or L. Venkataraman. Shops were more likely to sell tambaku paan in place of betel leaves and Chedi brand tobacco. Navratri would be celebrated with garbha dance in place of the south Indian kolu. He knew a few Marwaris well, and wondered how they felt to be suddenly alienated. He wondered how Tamilians in Delhi or Bombay would feel if the locals turned against them. He had read about some protests against South Indians in Maharashtra. Would there be a time when people stopped identifying friends and foes on the basis of state borders and started looking upon their countrymen as Indians? He reined in these random thoughts as the convoy reached the trouble spot. His watch read 12.35 pm as they swung into the street. And unknown to him, somewhere atop, a ledger book was being turned, his name found, and an instruction conveyed... by the Lord of Death, Yama, to his deputy, Chitragupt. Kumaramangalam's time had come.

* * *

Where were the protesters? Had the police arrived too late? Or was it a peaceful protest that could turn violent on sighting authority? Kumaramangalam knew from experience that government property and representatives of the State in any form were often the target during such agitations.

All the information the HQ had received was a message from the Sowcarpet police station – a radio message from a harried inspector saying the station was surrounded by more than 300 activists. The last sounds the HQ operator heard were slogans of protest and the transmission had ended abruptly.

No pedestrians on the street. Not even a stray dog in sight. An uneasy calm. Two streets to go to reach the police station, located adjacent to a public park, a few large houses, and down the street from a soda factory, ice cream maker and a petrol bunk, Kumaramangalam recalled from memory.

He hoped and prayed the protest would be peaceful. Soda bottles from the factory and petrol from the bunk - a lethal Molotov cocktail: Dip cotton into petrol, stuff on top of an open soda bottle, set fire to the cotton and toss the bottle in the air at the police. The gas within, compressed by the cotton and agitated by the bottle tossing and turning in the air would cause the bottle to explode, spreading smithereens of glass at high velocity.

One street more, left and then right, the convoy now face to face with a bloodcurdling sight: Over 3,000 protestors, not 300, lining the street and crowding the park, with placards and anti-government cries. His heart reached out to the five-member force manning the station. He knew the inspector well: Venkatesh, father of two sons and a daughter.

"Sir, the crowd is too large, what shall we do?" was the plea from his driver, Mathivanan, as they crossed the soda factory.

His men were grossly outnumbered by the crowd. The wireless operator must have scribbled the number wrong on his pad, he reckoned. The crowd was about 500 yards away, unaware of the approaching convoy. Must think, plan, only then act. The safety of his men would depend on his decision. Kumaramangalam raised his hand, bringing the convoy to a screeching halt.

Over a hundred protesters at the tailend turn around at the sound. Word passes down the line and soon over 6000 eyes are focused on the representatives of authority. Both groups take stock. The protesters are sure this small contingent would not be able to disperse them with a lathi charge, but the question is, are more reinforcements en route? Kumaramangalam wonders whether the crowd knows that help would never reach in time, if they were attacked.

"Sir, should we go back?" His junior from the jeep behind, now at his side, asks. Kumaramangalam turns grim-faced at the inspector, and scans the anxious faces of the posse awaiting his command, and his jeep driver, Mathivanan.

"Not till I find out what happened to Venkatesh and his men."

Tense, yet calm on the exterior, the lion from Tanjore picks up the loud hailer.

"Clear the way, we want to drive through, to the police station."

The crowd is defiant, and a menacing rumble emanates from its body. Faces, faces, faces glare at him. He feels no hatred towards them, they are his own people, from every walk of life, gathered together for what they believe is a worthy cause. He must do his duty and ensure his team's safety.

A clean-shaven young man with horn-rimmed spectacles emerges on the frontline. Apparently a leader, or one of the protest organizers.

"You can't see them. They are all behind bars in their own station."

"I have to find out if they are safe. If anything has happened to them, none of you will live."

"Challenging us are you?" If you have so much courage, drop your gun, and come with me to the station. I will show you. But only you can come. And your convoy has to retreat to the next street and wait till you come back. If they stay here, I cannot guarantee what this crowd will do. You know what we know. The police are outnumbered at least 20 times."

"Sir, don't listen, it's a trap. They will take you hostage. Please sir!"

The sound of a revolver dropping to the ground. Kumaramangalam removes his hat and places it on the jeep bonnet. "I trust you, and God above. Let's go."

Like the Red Sea, the crowd parts, as leader and inspector walk through the street and into the police station. There is only one man in the cell, Venkatesh.

"Where are the others?" Kumaramangalam asks the lone officer.

"They pleaded for their lives and ran away," the leader from behind answers the question. "Only this man is like you. He stood his ground."

Kumaramangalam has no time to relish the compliment. His mind is on full alert, framing the right sentences that can take them out of the jam.

"Now, I am going to take Venkatesh with me. If you maintain peace as we leave, we will not take any action. You have trespassed on government property, committed the offence of wrongful confinement, and the entire protest is against the prohibitory orders in force. But so far, the rally has remained peaceful and I acknowledge your leadership and discipline. Let the officer come with me, and we will not press charges."

Show no fear, keep talking, tough but sensibly, and you will live to relive this day, urges an inner voice. The odds are against you, you were foolish to attempt this rescue, warns another, but it is too late to reverse time. A hero dies only once, you were born to face such challenges, encourages another. Keep talking, cut the thoughts, warns another.

"You are a brave man, inspector. Take the other officer and leave now. I will see that no one lays a hand on you."

Kumaramangalam and Venkatesh, two of the finest officers of the Tamil Nadu police force, step out into the warm mid-morning sun, head held high. The crowd roars protesting their freedom. The student leader raises his hand. His charisma quells the sound.

Over 200 excruciating steps to reach the jeep. Now a hundred more. All the duo can see is a lone vehicle, no driver. Still there is hope, reckons Kumaramangalam, for a peaceful exit. Twenty steps more. Even his nerves of steel cannot control the hastening of his stride. Pray, pray, that there are no rebels, no claimants to the leadership. Hope, against all odds, I will return safe to the warm embrace of Marakatham, to a life of joy with little Arjun. Cut the thoughts, be alert! One last step, and swing into the jeep. The cold steering wheel is warm to the touch. There is no time to turn around, he has to reverse 100 yards into a lane perpendicular to the street, to the gates of the ice cream factory, and drive out on the road to freedom. The familiar crank of the starting motor, once, twice, three times. Oh please, fire, fire, he pleads with the ignition. Two lives rest on one spark. Sputter, chugh, vroom, the jeep starts with a reassuring, protective roar. Let in the clutch, gear in reverse, Venkatesh is tense by his side, his whole life ahead of him. Fifty yards in backward motion to the perpendicular street, he can smell the vapour of milk from the ice cream maker. Brake at the gate, first gear and sharply turn the steering wheel to the left. But they are not alone. Over a hundred protesters are running towards the jeep, not heeding the orders of the student leader. Either a splinter group, or a bunch of hooligans with a diabolical plan to plunder life and property. They know he does not have a revolver, they have seen it drop to the ground. Nothing like a burnt jeep and two battered policemen to send a harsh message to the government.

Engine in first gear, vehicle swarmed by people. "Kumar! Ram them with the jeep, hit two and the rest will scatter," urges Venkatesh. Survival of the toughest. Foot down on the accelerator, quick change to second gear, engine on high revs, the jeep surges ahead, causing three or four to jump aside to prevent being mowed down. "Keep going Kumar, these fellows are cowards." Kumaramangalam sees ahead a second life, a new beginning.

At that very moment, in the divine pen that chronicles Kumaramangalam's life on a celestial page, the ink begins to dry out. An unseen hand signs his death warrant with the last few drops. And on the ground, events unravel to reach the predestined end.

The engine sputters, once, twice and stops. As the powerless jeep grinds to a halt, Kumaramangalam plays his last card, an ace taped to his calf. "Venkatesh, as I get down, I am going to shoot, to disperse the mob. You just run, I am coming right behind you."

Venkatesh is too well trained to argue and waste precious moments. Just for a golden moment, he looks into Kumaramangalam's eyes, in the next fraction the agile officers are on hard ground. There is no time to warn, no time to shoot below the legs. He must kill at least two, to scatter 20. Boom! One man down, Boom! Another bites the dust, but the mob is multiplying. Third shot, he misses, nicking the target on the shoulder. Two more shots, direct hit on two hearts. Venkatesh's escape route is now being cut off. He turns and runs back towards Kumaramangalam. Only one bullet left, only one way out: Run for safety, run for life.

"Into the ice cream factory, Venkatesh." They dart into the compound, rush into the factory, past the curious workers. He can hear the gates clang shut, the security guards must be brave.

"Sir, this way sir, hide in the back, in the ice cream making area," says the factory manager or supervisor, he does not know who, but a good human being amid evil ones.

"Sir, before they break open the gate, take off your uniform, change into these overalls. Just mix with our people, we will tell them you escaped through the back door. We just have to manage the crowd till help arrives," a gallant man, this manager.

"Here sir, take these clothes." Without thinking, Kumaramangalam and Venkatesh reach for their tunic buttons. Even as the first two come off, their thoughts converge, transmitting by telepathy an admirable tenet: A just, upright policeman never discards his uniform.

"We are police officers. We are on duty. Let them take our lives, but our uniform will remain." Kumaramangalam is the first to speak. The manager is taken aback at the decision and at the firm tone, but has no time to reason why.

"Sir, go into the deep freeze, it is the only place where you can hide." He leads them through the factory into its bowels, and ultimately into the room where ice cream is set and stored in large horizontal bins at a temperature below zero.

The upholders of the law crouch behind the bins on the far side, choosing positions away from each other. Outside the gates, the noble student leader lies in a pool of blood, overpowered by death-hungry hooligans. Two handcarts from the street substitute for a battering ram. Break open the gates, burst into the factory, ravage the premises, scream for revenge. No sign of the two policemen. They have escaped through the back, claim the staff. More anger, more screams, more rampage. Shatter the place that gave them shelter, orders a hooligan. Overturn milk cans, bang the metal on machines, smash chairs on tables, break glass, loot the cash box, let loose anarchy.

"Throw out all the ice cream on the road, destroy the full stock. This factory must never help a policeman again." Now into the deep freeze, pull out bins of ice cream – chocobar sticks, strawberry cups, bright orange sticks, vanilla in white plastic balls with blue caps, throw every flavour, and order out.

"Dai, parunga, there is a policeman hiding here." Venkatesh

is discovered, crouching in a corner. Drag him by the collar. Kumaramangalam unobserved under a heap of black polyethylene canopy. Stay quiet, you will live, in this frenzy they will not look for the other man. No, Venkatesh must be saved, whatever may be the cost. Kumaramangalam rises with a war cry and pumps a bullet at point blank range into the man who is holding Venkatesh by the throat. The mob within the deep freeze stares askance. No one wants to die, no one knows how many guns and bullets this policeman has. Kumaramangalam lifts the gun again.

"One more step, I will shoot all of you dead. Let us go, I will spare you." Brave, very brave. This is the reason he was born: to face danger in its face. No one wants to call his bluff. He holds Venkatesh by his left arm, gun raised on the other, and exits the deep freeze, head held high.

Odds are odds. When they are stacked against you, luck will ultimately run out. A milk can missile is thrown from behind at Venkatesh, causing a gash on his scalp. Chairs travel towards them like arrows. As they buckle down, twenty pairs of hands of hold them tight.

They are handcuffed with rope, led out into the hot daylight. Each of them is lashed to a handcart, bleeding, spread-eagled. They are wheeled amid a hooting mob to the public park, adjacent to the petrol bunk. They are doused with inflammable fuel from chest to toe. From the corner of his eye, Kumaramangalam can see a man running out of a house, a bright veil around his face, a burning stick of wood in his hand. Roars of revenge reverberate as the flame holder nears the live pyres.

"I am sorry Venky, I did my best," are his last words. The mind replays rich images of past and present: Marakatham on their wedding night, Arjun in the crib, his father and mother in the verandah of their ancestral home in Kumbakonam… oh God, there is so much more. The petrol on his soaked skin ignites as the hooligan torches his tunic. Pain, unbearable pain, as the flesh singes. Lashed to the cart, he cannot even writhe, grant the body its reflex reaction to pain.

"Please, please, mother, take me away, I cannot bear it anymore… Water, Waterrrr!" he screams, involuntarily opening his parched mouth. The man with the bright veil now has a bottle in his hand. Maybe the devil's way of fulfilling a death wish.

Mouth open to the sky, the dry tongue awaits salvation while the lower body burns. Devil pours from the bottle. Clear, crystal clear... crystal clear ... kerosene, splashing on his face, racing down the throat. The burning stick torches his face, and in a second the larynx and lungs within.

His last vision... evil eyes above the veil, watching him writhe in agony. Pain, unbearable pain, as life exits flesh. Peace, everlasting peace. Amidst a madding crowd, end, lonely end.

* * *

CHAPTER FOUR

Not even monastery walls,

not even the remoteness of the desert,

can defend against the female presences;

for as long as the hermit's flesh

clings to his bones, and pulses warm,

the images of life are alert to storm his mind.

He lived alone, but the past could never leave him alone. During all the years he had lived abroad, he had never had roommates, or stayed as a houseguest of another family. He knew they would never understand or accept his silence, sudden turnoffs, and occasional bouts of lightheartedness. There were no women in his life, although some had been attracted by his good looks and melancholy demeanour, finding him a better alternative to men who talked non-stop about themselves. He had never provided encouragement, or a hint that he would like to foster their interest. Only two women got through the iron curtain.

One lived in the apartment opposite his. Her husband was an Indian businessman from South Africa who had decided to make the US his base, fearing further political unrest and economic upheaval in the Continent. He travelled frequently, because of expanding markets, and because he could not successfully remote control his African enterprises.

Back to the protagonist. He hardly spoke to her during the first year. He would run into her at the elevator, nod at her at the pool, and sometimes see her when he returned from his morning run, seated by the French window, sipping her morning tea, dressed in a soft pink or mellow yellow housecoat. She was tall, big made and well rounded, yet carried her large frame gracefully. Somehow, her solid appearance gave him a sense of inner comfort.

As it happens often in our lives, one thing led to another, and the young man finally had occasion to speak to her. It was wintertime in Boulder. He had been away on work in New York for two weeks, returned home late at night, travel weary and hungry. The fridge was empty, with not even lettuce and butter to make a decent sandwich. He did not fancy heating up the only TV dinner lying in the freezer. Hunger was about the only thing that could overcome his reserve.

He knocked at her door and asked her if she could give him a cup of rice. He planned to mix the rice with buttermilk, add pickle for taste, and make a meal of it. To his relief, she suggested that he drop in for dinner, if only he could wait for 20 minutes. He had a quick shower, changed into a pullover and track bottoms, and returned to her apartment. Watching her bustling about the kitchen, noting her happiness in setting the table, he realised it was not just she, but a nation's culture at work - upholding the cherished tradition of Indian hospitality that makes a guest welcome anywhere in the world.

Thirty minutes later, he was gratefully deep into a meal of hot puris, palak paneer, dal and steaming basmati rice. She was apologetic about the paneer and dal for they were a carryover from lunch, yet he found the flavour sublime, enhanced over time in the cold clime.

He discovered she was born in Cape Town, studied in London, and married at the age of 21. She said London had been her husband's base during the initial years of their marriage. They had a child, who was now studying in Australia. From the artifacts, paintings, curios, collector's items and collection of books in the living room, he deduced they loved art, were well read, and had traveled widely. He wanted to ask her what she had studied in London, but decided against it. He surmised she would have completed a course in interior decoration or some such thing women like to dabble in after marriage.

He discovered that they were alike. She never made small talk. She either collected information or disseminated it. As he was working on his ice cream with a tall spoon to stir the fruit and jelly at the bottom, he noticed that she had become silent, possibly because she had asked what she wanted to know.

"Is this Hagen Daz? No other brand has this rich taste. And the fresh fruits are heavenly." For him food talk was not small talk. It was critical conversation.

She smiled. She had always liked this quiet young man. It would not have been proper to tell him that. She had wanted to speak to him, find

45

out what kind of a person he was, for two reasons: One, he was from India, and knowing a countryman always came in handy when you were alone in a foreign land; two, he was so well built and good looking, one had to get to know him, not for ulterior reasons, but to test if his heart was as good as his body.

She knew he was a loner, because friends never dropped in, Indians or others. He looked so serious all the time, one would think twice before breaking the ice. Today, after the meal, he was relaxed, and cheerful. He looked better this way, she thought.

She did not tell her husband about the visitor when he returned the next week. He was a hard-core businessman, always toting up turnover figures in his many companies. He ate skimpy meals, rarely acknowledged the variety she cooked when he was in town, never expressed interest in what she had done during the day, and forever worried about his business overseas when he was in the United States. This time, she was quite happy to see him leave abruptly on the third day, to manage a payment crisis that had cropped up in Cape Town.

She actually stayed up several nights, hoping her solemn neighbour would knock again. It was silly, but deep within each of us we entertain such trivial but pleasant hopes, based on a single incident.

She called a South Indian friend in New York, asked her the dates of upcoming festivals. Pongal was just a few days away, the friend said. She asked her Indian grocer for a cookbook, but it did not have the recipe she wanted.

She spoke to her friend again, got her to fax the recipe, ordered jaggery, nutmeg and other ingredients from an Indian grocer in Boulder, and got the friend to courier by Fedex the special vessel to cook the traditional sweet dish.

On January 14th, at 7 a.m. while towelling himself dry after a long run and shower, he was surprised to hear the door chime. Presently, he opened the door to find no one, started closing it, wondering if it was a pesky kid playing pranks. His nose perked up at the aroma that was wafting in from the corridor. He opened the door again, sniffed, and found the source. To the left of his door, was a brass vessel, adorned with palm leaves at the steel plate. When it came to food, his motto was to eat first, ask questions later. He used a dishcloth to carry the hot container to his dining table.

He pushed aside the refined white bread and cornflakes that now seemed unnatural, compared to the ghee laden, nutmeg, raisin and cashew garnished, rice and jaggery preparation, served steaming hot, half way around the world, transporting him back in time to his mother's kitchen.

Only after he disposed of more than half of the sweet pongal did he think of wandering around for clues. He found a note slipped under the door. She had written it out with a red felt pen, on her feminine, personal letterhead. "Happy Pongal. Hope it's half as good as what your mother would have made back home. Neelam."

After that, there was no ice to break. He ate at her place once a week on Friday nights, and one Sunday morning they had lunch at an Indian restaurant downtown. Matters came to a head on a Saturday evening, when his washing machine broke down. She spotted him from the French window, walking towards the condo's laundromat with a basket of clothes. Five minutes later, he was in the utility room of her apartment. He set the controls, poured detergent on the load, and settled down with a book in one corner. He was always intrigued by the hum of the washing machine, the staccato cycle that would soak the clothes, the sound of water gushing in and receding, and the final spin that would wring out the water and send out the suds. From start to finish, it was a cleansing act, and for some strange reason, he liked being close to it.

"Why don't you have a shower and come back? I have already made dinner," she announced, not giving him much of a choice. To prolong his visit, she switched the TV channel to a Bond film rerun, and he lingered on after dinner watching it.

"Would you like to have a drink... brandy, sherry, liqueur?"

"No, please no. I don't drink, ever."

"All right, I am sure you will have some cappuccino. Not like your filter stuff, but any coffee lover will like it."

He had never had cappuccino before. He found the taste strange, but drank it anyway, not wanting to offend his hostess. He was seated on

47

her divan, and on her insistence, stretched his long legs, resting his back against the soft cushions. He had run 2 hours 20 minutes that morning, and was feeling sleepy. He could hear her talking to him, asking him something, and that was the last thing he heard that night.

He woke at 5 a.m., something he always did, winter or summer, without the help of an alarm. His mouth had a flat taste, and his head felt heavy. He realized with a jolt that he was not in his apartment. He panicked for a moment, but regained his composure, for he recalled doing nothing wrong. Groggy, thirsty and confused, he wandered to the kitchen for a glass of water. She had forgotten to put back the brandy in its place. He saw the bottle and knew the rest.

He turned around to see her at the kitchen door. She was wearing a white satin robe. She was still tying the waistband, for she must have woken up just after he did.

"I told you I don't drink. Why did you put liquor in my coffee?"

"Because I wanted you to loosen up. I want to know the thoughts that reverberate in that mind of yours. I asked you questions as you were drifting off, and you answered some of them. Now, I know you in and out."

"What did you ask? What did I say?" He was almost in tears, because for the first time someone had cut through his reticence.

She smiled. Came close. Encircled her arms around his broad shoulders, her fingers resting on the nape of his neck. "Arjun, you said you would marry me."

* * *

Never propose to a married woman. Consciously or otherwise. That may very well have been the moral of the brandy episode. The truth was her revelation brought hem closer, and tore him apart. Sure, he had found her attractive, enjoyed being with her, savoured her culinary skills. And other than his work, she had been the only link to the present.

Startled by her statement, and fascinated by the novel experience of a woman's arms encircling him, he remained transfixed, heart warning him to break away, body wanting to stay put. Her large frame, flowing

48

mane, and well-filled contours lulled all sense of propriety. Only when he noticed the amusement in her eyes, did he stiffen and draw away.

"You are pulling a fast one."

"I am serious, Arjun dear. You said what you said."

"I did not intend it. I am sorry."

This time, she just held his hand. "The mind runs amok sometimes. Some of our thoughts are fantasies, some wishful thinking, and a rare few are the converse statement of a long nurtured want. Your problem is you talk to nobody. From your lonely existence, I know there is a longing somewhere. You like that part of me... fussing over you. In your subconscious, there is a girl tucked away. I can see that. What you did, when you spoke from your subconscious, was to satiate two desires in one stroke: your longing for marriage and motherhood."

From mutter paneer to psychoanalysis. This was a huge jump. It is in our habit to stereotype people; he had labeled her as just the wife of a rich businessman.

He looked at her with new respect. He saw her as the personification of the true Indian woman, who could give so much of her soul to a man, and play multiple roles in life: as wife, mother and true friend.

* * *

Arjun had just one person he could call a friend. She lived thousands of miles away, yet qualified as a close friend with whom he shared a warm relationship.

It all started at a Durga Puja function organised by the Bengali Association of Boulder. The chief guest, Ms. Rekha Sen, West Bengal's most admired actress in the late 1970s. Arjun had been a reluctant guest. He had turned up only because his colleague Biswas had lured him with the promise of succulent rosagollas and other sweet delights from the East. And assured him he would not have to socialize, but could leave immediately after dinner, dessert to be precise.

Because he wanted to be unobtrusive, because he wanted to avoid attention, he happened to be the only one among the 50 plus gathering who did not exchange words or at least greet Rekha Sen during the tete-a-tete with the star, immediately after the puja, just before dinner. She was surprised and curious because a man who would not take a second look at her was rare. It could mean a hundred fans could dismiss her when the comeback vehicle she was dreaming about came true. She could not afford to lose attention on screen or off it. To cut a long story short, she was not used to being ignored.

Well, the truth was that he was hungry, not interested in visiting dignitaries, because such people by nature of their fleeting presence, would not make any difference to his life (he had noticed her good looks, and well-preserved figure, but she wouldn't know that).

During dinner, at the dessert counter, she asked the secretary of the association about the quiet visitor who was by now busy with a large helping of sondesh. The secretary did not know, but he asked Biswas, who promptly introduced Arjun to her. Arjun said hello, and apologetically added that he had heard about her only that evening. He said he was from South India and his knowledge of Bengali cinema was limited to Satyajit Ray and Uttam Kumar. After that he did not know what to say, so he stood silent, not wanting to make small talk, which impressed her more.

She had wanted to be sought after, but now she sought to know him. She guessed he was a confirmed bachelor. A man in his late 30s who was so quiet with a beautiful woman had to be, had to have shunned women all through adulthood. She guessed he was celibate too, and that strangely excited her. She had to get closer to this shy Madrasi dada.

As he was working his spoon through two plump rossogollas, she drew him aside. "Mr. Arjun, I am being felicitated tomorrow at the Indian Cultural Centre. Clips of some of my films will be screened as part of the function. Please be my guest."

She wanted him to know her background, name and fame as an actress. She was obsessed with being well known, and here was one (strapping, muscular) man who had to be inducted into her fan club.

To her surprise, he did land up the next day, tagging along with Biswas. She was glad he was present to watch the special feature that chronicled her ascent, from a small time actress to a star. It had first been aired on Calcutta Doordarshan, and every aspect it showcased was what she wanted the world to know, and shared with the interviewer. She was the daughter of a clerk who toiled for years in a government office in Asansol. They lived in a three-room apartment. Her brother took after her father, and she was the dreamy one, aspiring for the glamour of tinsel world.

The film would not reveal what she would always conceal, the compromises in the early part of her career, the slow distancing of her conservative family, and the heroes who played the villain roles in her life. Along with fame came money, a house in Ballygunge and loneliness.

He was glad he had come for the event, because as he watched the film clips, one coherent thought was taking shape in his focussed mind: Click! In a flash, he knew why he wanted to see more of her.

His casual interest in the actress since yesterday would now turn into an active pursuit. Much to her surprise, and satisfaction, he approached her after the screening, and asked for her address. He also shyly enquired if she would send him a photo of hers from time to time. She accepted, thrilled to have won his admiration. If only she could get to know him better before leaving Boulder…

His thoughts were echoing hers. Just a postal or electronic relationship would not suffice. He had to get closer to her, capture, retain and savour her image. He was not skilled in converting a casual acquaintance into a close friend, but this time he would try hard.

"Miss Sen, you must be having quite a schedule, what with the entire Bengali community wanting to meet you and ready to offer you any assistance. Still… if you can spare some time for me, there is one place I would like to take you to." Ah, she mused, even the saint could not remain indifferent to her. He would invite her to dinner, hopefully in candlelight, and a drink or two in his masculine company would be just right to elevate her spirits. She was sure he would be less inhibited if she could coax him into having more than his due. She had the right outfit for such an occasion.

"The place I would like to take you to, tomorrow if you are free," he continued, "is a very special temple, a few hours drive from Boulder."

* * *

She looked five years younger, and a shade lighter and fitter, in the morning light. Dark brown corduroy trousers hugging her lower body, not too tight, but fitting pat, a pair of light brown Adidas shoes, light cream round neck vest tucked into the pants, matching corduroy jacket with flapped pockets. No bindi on her forehead. Tresses loose and blowing free in the cool Colorado breeze. Sun glasses and a warm smile.

He took her travel bag and stored it in the boot, alongside his. It was a four hour drive to the temple, and chances were they would be back only late in the night, allowing for an hour at the temple and another hour or more for stopovers.

She climbed into the seat beside him and snuggled in deep. "Can you help me with the seat belt, young man? I can never draw the belt in one sweep."

As he reached over to the left, and pulled the metal clasp diagonally over her, taking care not to touch her with his fingers or the belt, he caught a whiff of her perfume. Unlike the dinner night, she hardly had any make up on, just a touch of lipstick. She had a firm, clear complexion and the rest of her was in good shape too. Must be the fish. He fastened his seat belt next, and started the engine, looking forward to the company of this mature woman.

The drive was safe and uneventful. Unlike the Indian highway, where the probability of colliding with a car, lorry, or variety of other animate or inanimate objects is very high, the American interstate highway, or Turnpike as it is called, offers zero chances of head on collision, unless of course a rookie driver has decided to drive in the wrong direction while reentering from an exit or truck stop. The highway is divided, two lanes or more for upcoming traffic and likewise for traffic moving downward. Accidents of course were likely to happen due to other reasons – over-speeding, driving under the influence of alcohol, following too closely or any other kind of improper judgment. Such being the backdrop, driving in the United States, especially on a Turnpike, is bliss. Driving with a beautiful Bengali woman added bliss.

52

On their way up, they had settled for a light snack in place of lunch at a Wendys. They reached the motel about 3 pm and he spotted a Dunkin Donuts store, which had a reputation for serving fresh coffee. "I am dying for a cup of strong coffee," he announced, adding as an afterthought, "How about you?"

"Dying too, but for a cup of tea," she retorted with a smile. Inexplicable... he was beginning to like this mature woman, far removed from his social and ethnic context.

"We would have to be at the temple by 4 pm for the darshan, I have rented a room for a few hours, since you wanted to freshen up and change... after tea, why don't you check in, I will wait at the lobby, you go up, I follow in 10 minutes."

"Ji Sarkar, just as you say."

He waited for 15 minutes, just to give her enough leeway, and then took the elevator to the fourth floor, Room 432. As the car traveled upward, he pondered over his new-found companion. From knowledge and from personal experience, he knew the attitude of Indian visitors toward NRIs. While in the US, they tended to be extremely grateful to the hosts, and their departure would always be marked by invitations to their home in India, and promises for any assistance the NRI may need. Some would send a thank you letter on reaching home; a few would keep in touch every year with greeting cards. The majority couldn't care once they were on the plane. He expected a similar treatment from the actress, who in any case, would not know the reason why he fancied her. She was the epitome of preservation, and in his mind, a torchbearer of hope, because if this woman at 40 could be well preserved... then the chiffon girl could.

As was often the case, thoughts of the girl from the past put him into a trance, and it was a spellbound young man who reached the door of Room No. 432 oblivious of reality, and etiquette such as knocking before entry. The door was ajar. He did not consciously make a move to enter, but his palm, guided by a command from deep within pushed the door gently. The deserted motel, the woman in the room, and the knowledge she was dressing within, triggered from the unconscious a long-forgotten memory, and turned him into a mesmerized object.

What is forbidden is ecstasy. Ambrosia is a woman semi clad. In a dark blue petticoat and light blue blouse, with her back to him. Her head was down, and her hands seemed busy, possibly uniting hooks under strain. The skin on her back was pure and fresh, not one blemish. Her lower body had an hourglass contour, narrow at the waist, billowing slightly below. His life would never be the same again, his soul would boil in hell forever, yet, for that moment, impending punishment was no deterrent.

In a world full of pre-marital and extra-marital affairs, in a world of Bohemian couples, if his sin was intrusion of privacy, so be it. As he watched spellbound, logic presented a new reasoning: Her figure was a work of art, placing him under aesthetic arrest, permitting him to contemplate and enjoy. To admire her beauty was not an indulgence, but an act of reverence. One step further, if his admiration turned into desire, and desire into lust, then awe would descend into pornography.

She seemed to have won her battle with the hooks, for she now picked up a starched cotton saree from the bed and proceeded to adorn it, expertly and efficiently, with measured folds and accurate inserts of the fabric into the waistline. Next, the folding of the saree top and the drape across the shoulder and breasts. She draped once, was not satisfied, gathered differently, and draped it again. Swiftly, she turned 180 degrees, and faced the door: "How does it look Arjun?"

"Uh, huh, sorry, I was just coming in." Breathless. Remorseful. Wave of admiration washed out by guilt.

"Arjun da! Aap abhi aaye? I saw you in the mirror two minutes ago, who was that, your humshakal, or your dupe?"

"Ah, er, no, me only. I forgot to knock, you were busy, so I was waiting. Shall I go and come back?" He just wanted to disappear in a puff of smoke.

"I am not hurt, so you don't have to feel so bad. I have dressed and undressed enough times in front of the camera, so these things don't mean anything any more. Why don't you come in, sit, and you can tell me whether I am getting my make-up right. I don't want to go into the temple like a doll, just a bit of foundation, a dash of lipstick, and I will be done."

She put her arm around his shoulder, led him to the bed and seated him on the mattress. Her saree fabric touched the bachelor's face for a nanosecond. Numbed by the experience, yet mind craving for more, his gaze shifted to the dressing table, where she had picked up a jar of pink colored cream. She spread the cream on her face, smoothening it across the cheeks and then toning down the colour with a pad of foam. Next, she produced a hairbrush from her kit, and proceeded to brush with long strokes. A routine effort for her, but a sensuous act for the innocuous observer perched on the bed. First she brushed the mane from behind while allowing it to rest across her shoulders, then pushed the tresses fully on to her left shoulder, and brushed hard the curls at the end in an attempt to straighten them. She placed the brush on the dressing table, and in a flash gathered the soft, thick hair and fastened it with a clip that she had held between her teeth. A lipstick found its way to her luscious lips, and she was ready.

She looked at Arjun and waved her hand in front of his eyes: "I am just an old woman, acting young. The way you are looking at me, I will begin to believe I am still attractive."

"Actually you are. You are timeless, if you would let me say it... like Cleopatra," he said hesitantly.

"Well, well, that sounds flattering. If I remember right, Cleopatra was known for answering one's most passionate demands and, in the process of satisfying one's desires, she could reawaken them.

"Sadly, I have been doing that on screen for years, satisfying other's desires, but I never could transcend from the make-believe stage to something real and permanent. For my male fans, I was a substitute in their fantasies; female fans would see themselves in me, to fill in the glamorous life that they would never get to enjoy.

"Everyone I met has been a visitor, a guest in my life. I have had no deep-rooted friendships, because people wanted from me short-term gains - the producer wanted a hit film, the writer would want to pen an award winning role, and the heroes wished to pair with me as long as I was successful at the box office.

"Wonder why I am speaking in a frank manner, all of a sudden? When you were watching me, I thought you had ulterior motives.

When I escorted you to the bed, it was a test, and had you attempted to take advantage, I would have known you were just another lustful man. I realized your intentions were honourable. You love women, and you rarely get a chance to express your admiration for them overtly." Atonement for a distant sin. Reassurance of virtue. Proof that life could come in a full circle. He has no time to think further, for she now has stepped closer and hugged him tight.

Neelam, now Sen. Why did it feel so good? Was it because a woman's flesh against the body felt so heavenly? Or beyond the physical, was it reversal of emotion - relishing their presence because they liked being with him?

"Now, don't get me wrong. This is an emotional hug, not a passionate one," he could hear her saying, her right fist gently squeezing the firm muscle below the shoulder blade. Too good, the onus was on her to stop, having started it. "Just want to say you are a true gentleman, although a slightly confused one. Let us move on, it's time to go to the temple, there's a lifetime ahead to discover more about each other."

As they came apart, he wasn't too sure what the last statement meant, but he was already on a high for two reasons: Watching her dress, unashamedly, was one, and the second was the proximity that had developed, unexpectedly, within the last few minutes.

The temple visit was uneventful. The crowd was thin, Lord Balaji adorned in jewels and decked in sandal paste was magnificent, and the darshan heart warming. They returned to the motel, she changed back to Western attire, and this time he stayed at the lobby till she checked out. Within five minutes they were on the Turnpike heading for Boulder.

Rekha Sen opened her handbag, frowning for a few seconds, then experienced a flood of relief. A pack of Virginia Slims emerged followed by a lighter.

"Can I lower the window glass just a little bit?" I am not a regular smoker, but once a while I enjoy a drag," she said, placing a cigarette on her lips.

"How about you Arjun, do you smoke?"

"Uh, huh, I don't."

"Do you drink?"

"Oh, never."

"What about sex?"

Here was a woman different from the others. Not tepid, withdrawn or conservative like the girl; not interactive or understated like Neelam; but broad-minded, candid and overt. Traits possibly shaped by a career in the no-holds-barred world of celluloid.

Startled at first, recovering fast, he had not minded her rapid-fire quiz. Yet, he consciously assumed a hurt, rued expression, ruling it to be the warranted emotion for such an unusual barrage.

It was Rekha Sen who broke the silence. "Sorry, I couldn't resist hooking you with that one," she said, and added with a twinkle in her eye. "I stand guilty, and ready for any penalty that you may desire to impose."

"I was thinking of that too," he retorted with a smile. "There's an exit in five minutes, the verdict is... cinnamon rolls and coffee."

* * *

A fortnight after her return to Calcutta, she wrote to him a brief thank you note, enclosing her autographed photograph. The interaction that followed puzzled her.

Arjun never drooled, yet his attention never waned. Through his letters, later emails, she felt his gaze was always on her. Through the photos she sent, he was constantly updating his vision of her, and for some reason, more than information on her routine and chores, her visual image seemed to matter most. She did not take offence, for as an actress, she was used to adoring eyes; she also acknowledged that looks were her best asset. With Arjun, it hurt because for a person so deep, he never wished to delve into her mind.

Somewhere towards the end of the first year of their postal and e-mail relationship, after she received his 12th or 13th communication, and after sending him her 8th or 9th recent photograph, she had started nearing, rather fearing the truth about Arjun. Her feminine intuition said he feared her discovery too, because he was beginning to alter the content and focus of his letters dramatically, or not ask for her photograph even after two months. He was desperately and deliberately going on a tangent, because he feared the woman in her would sense his direction. Time for an acid test. She called in her long-time make up man and hair dresser, made changes to her appearance, and mailed her photograph, with a note that said: "Me as I am today. Hope you will still write."

His response, or lack of it, would confirm her worst fear: That she was a dupe, for the heroine living in his heart.

* * *

There were many reasons why he liked living in the condominium. It was located in the outskirts of Boulder, which meant he could chalk out long, lonely running routes without running into people or vehicles. The occupancy rate was less than 50%, which meant less people to meet and greet. The icing really, in ice-cold Boulder, was the condo's heated, sparingly used gymnasium, open round the clock.

His routine: finish the morning run and land up at the gym by 6.30 a.m., fully warmed up, loosened up and raring to go. He had a definite exercise plan for every day. Tuesdays – ground exercises, meaning freehand exercises without any aids such as weights, skipping rope or bench. The masochist in Arjun insisted he always start with the toughest exercise dreaded even by the fittest soldier: Commando Push-ups. Body parallel to the exercise mat, palms placed on the surface, lift the body with the power of the arms, and then the clincher… raise palms in the air, clap once and palms back to the mat before the chest can hit the surface. A tough army commando would manage five of these, but for a man looking for outlets to vent his angst, the satiation level was ten.

Wednesday was his weight training day. He preferred light weights with high repetitions, to build power rather than muscle.

Thursdays were special. Because that was circuit training day, an exercise that is aerobic in nature. Circuit training is patterned after ground exercises, except that the sets are performed at a faster pace with no gap during changeover - one exercise moves on to another, and another, until the trainee completes his designated "circuit" of exercises. Guaranteed to take the heart rate to 180 and leave you panting like a steam engine moving at peak speed. Two minutes break for the heart to slow down to 120, then one full circuit again, break, and the last circuit.

It was at the end of his third circuit on a Thursday morning that Neelam found him, as she strolled into the gym, dressed in tights and a tight fitting T-shirt. The sight of her, and her clearly outlined contours increased his heart rate further.

"Hello, young man, You have inspired me with your daily running. I came in to jog on the treadmill." The gym had a computerised treadmill, but Arjun did not fancy it, resorting to its use just once, on a day that Boulder recorded its highest snowfall in 50 years. He preferred to run in the open, thoughts running through his mind, mind running through his past.

"Hello, hello, stop drooling, start teaching me how to exercise properly. I thought exercise made the body supple. Last two days I have been working out at home, but I feel so stiff."

"Well, well, well," he drawled. "Maybe you should go easy on the sherry, why blame the exercise? Ok, ok, don't glare at me, I was just kidding."

"Other things being equal, I would say your problem is stretching, rather the lack of it. The golden rule is 'warm up, warm down.' Which means you have to stretch sufficiently before and after."

"Teach me guru, and ask for any *dakshina* you want," she said, with a twinkle in her eye.

"Sizzling hot Pongal would be fine. If you can cut the corn, we can get down to business. I will now initiate you into the art of stretching, but it demands a pledge. Only if you take the pledge, you can pass to the next level, wherein you will be initiated into the art."

"Guruji, joh aap kahenge, woh hum karenge."

"Er, what was that, you cursing me?"

"You guys never learnt Hindi all your life? I am saying I submit to you totally. Aage bado… I am ready for the pledge."

"Stand straight, look into my eyes, what's this, I see mirth and not seriousness. Come on now, chin up, don't let your shoulders droop, chest out, stand ramrod straight, ahem, take it easy, your instructor is losing balance. Let's get on with it. We are ready for the pledge. Raise your right hand, state your name at length and repeat after me."

"Hey, hey what's this? Some ancient rite or precursor to sorcery?"

"Trust me. Repeat your name at length and say it after me. I – your name please!"

"I, Dr. Neelam Gupta, oops, plain Neelam Gupta, do hereby and solemnly pledge that I will always stretch, before and after my exercise routine, be it aerobics, weight training, calisthenics, jogging, racquet games or any other form of physical exercise. This I solemnly pledge, without exception or equivocation."

"Great show, you may now drop your hand. Now we can start the initiation"

"You mean the pledge is over?"

"Yeah, what did you expect, that we would dance around a fire?"

"I am coming to the point, you nut... In ancient times, a pledge was required to be sealed with the lips on a sacred book, as a mark of fidelity. I was waiting for something like that," she said and stepped closer. "That's probably how the expression "my lips are sealed" came about. "Now, shall I seal my lips with yours?"

"Aiyo, vendaam!" he exclaimed, and jumped back two steps. Feet hit treadmill, he lost balance, regained momentarily and lost balance again when he could not find anything to hold on to. She reacted with amazing reflexes to break his fall, encircling her left arm around his waist and drawing him close. The danger had passed, but she continued to hold him, her eyes just three inches from his. What was it about this man she liked so much? Not just his physique – able-bodied men were not difficult to come by. Soft-hearted were. Involuntarily, her grip tightened, edging closer, breaking down his reluctance and resistance. She scanned his face for signs of passion or compassion. As the intimacy turned intense, as her involuntary senses demanded of her that she smother him, she realized she was crossing boundaries and heading towards a point of no return.

She drew away from him. It would be an insult if he did first. "Well, well, always remember I saved your life. Or at least a week in hospital. Now let us stop running around the treadmill and help me to run on it. Come on dear, set the machine for me."

The motor whirred as he set the treadmill in motion. He punched in walking speed, to enable her to warm up before breaking into a jog.

"OK, buster, I will walk, you talk. I will put forth a question, and you answer. First tell me, why are you so crazy... about keeping fit? I suspect you have a genetic problem."

"Well, you are close to the truth," he answered with a smile. "I sometimes wish I had joined the defence services or the police force like my father. Working in front of a computer is not my cup of tea, though it suffices for my daily bread. That's the reason why I make my mornings different from my day, that's how I manage to stay clear of the mundane.

Pumping iron or pumping the heart raises my adrenaline. I am happiest right in the midst of exercise, I look forward to that part after the first half hour when the body is all warmed up, the heart beats at a steady rhythm, and endorphins are at peak. I miss a work profile that would require me to be physically active through the day. Yet, I satiate the longing in an unusual way."

"I bet you go about torturing women. First you get friendly, then you torment!"

"For the cheek you have, you may be the first. What I do is this: While most people take a vacation once a year, and travel to exotic places, I trade my annual break for a survival course that challenges my fitness levels. The course organizers believe that I enroll to survive doomsday, and at least 40 others take part for that very reason.

"The course structure is unique, and would raise eyebrows even in army circles, being so gruelling. It is held every year in Nebraska, somewhere in a forest area. We are eight teams of five members each, and our challenge is to traverse 100 miles on foot in five days. We have a common starting point and each team follows a charted route, and rarely comes into contact with the other. The route is clearly

61

marked. What makes it difficult is the obstacles laid down on the way. Circumventing would mean disqualification. Torches are not permitted, no tents, no warm clothing beyond a basic cardigan. Canned food is placed at pre-marked dead drops, twice a day, at morning and night. We are not given any communication equipment and no help is provided by way of medical aid on the way, except in cases of fatal injury which can only be communicated by the team leader activating a radio signal in his back pack.

"We have to keep moving, run in fact, almost all day on difficult terrain. Sleep is for three hours, for resting more would mean we would not reach the finish by day five. The obstacles can take various forms, logs of wood placed en route, which would take us an hour to clear, with each team member helping to lift the logs and place them out of the way. Walking through slush, crawling through dense undergrowth, and swimming across a wide river. I have done it for three years, and from next year I will be the team leader.

"Listen, now it is my turn to ask, and if you can answer without breathing hard, it means you are walking speed is just right.

"Tell me about your husband, what does he do, what kind of a person is he."

"Well, his is a great immigrant story. His grandfather started off as a labourer in a diamond mine in South Africa. Slowly, he set out on his own, got a mine on lease, and that happened to hold a mother lode of diamonds. The mine passed on to the next generation and to my husband. My husband diversified into trading, and of late his company has entered into construction projects too, which is why he spends a lot of time in Africa."

"I would like to meet him when he comes in next time. Will you introduce me?"

She kept walking for sometime and signalled she was ready to move to the next level. He increased the speed one notch and waited for her to get used to the pace.

"If you are expecting a sociable person, you are going to be disappointed. He is quiet, thinks all the time about his business. Better brush up on world trade if you want to meet him."

He did not intend asking the next question, but in the secluded gymnasium, with the memory of their interaction the previous week, and her apparent comfort in his presence, the question slipped out:

"You don't talk much about him. I was wondering if... all is well..."

"Oh, you want to help me if all is not? I don't talk about him because whatever I tell you about him, will not interest you. First thing you must learn is a woman will rarely talk about her husband to another man, and most men do not want to know either, unless it is some negative info that they can leverage. Women will talk to other women, and they paint different kinds of pictures of their husband when they do: some will gush about their tender loving husband, and others will present them as oversexed maniac, miser, wife beater, man with a roving eye, the descriptions go on..."

"Since you are naïve in these matters, I will tell you something more. I am not likely to tell my husband too much about you. It is difficult to place our friendship in perspective to someone who drops in like a guest for a few days. Max, I will mention that you knocked the door hungry and I served you a hot meal. That's a story he would like to hear because hospitality is something our family takes pride in."

He did not back off, but plodded on towards something he wanted to affirm. "Listen, you need to keep your weight forward. Correct that by exaggerating the correction, lean forward almost as though you are stooping, and you can walk or run comfortably in that posture." With that bit of advice, he resumed his query.

"Ok, let me not ask you about him, but I will ask you about yourself, and this has no ulterior motive. Are you married to the right partner?"

"Honest answer: I am not. But you are going to find very few women who are. Marriage is like a trade, a give and take. Or like an exam. You get 35% you have passed, 60% is first class, and 75 is distinction, that's the Indian system right?" Likewise, I give my marriage a first class, because the man I am wedded to is kind, takes care of my wants and most important is not the snoopy, suspicious type. But I have gripes too, I had a career before we got married, but then he kept equating my work with money and would always point out that what I earned was peanuts compared to what his business makes, so why did I have to work? Then came our son, so finally I had to give up what I cherished most."

"What were you working as?"

"Well, I was helping people, you could say. People who had problems would come to me, and I would help them with some advice. You can call it counselling. It's too inconsequential to go into details... plus I don't think I can continue to talk and run at the same time. Put up the pace, let me see how long I can run."

* * *

At the end of 15 minutes, even at the moderate pace he has set, the big-made woman begins to wear out. He knows she would not collapse; she would not get out of bed next day either.

"Neelam madam, we are not doing a cardiac test here. If you want to stop, just tell me."

Just the cue she is waiting for. Even before he could caution her not to stop abruptly, but wait for him to wind down the belt speed, she punches the Stop button on the controls. Which is a mistake if you are not used to running on the treadmill. Your feet, tuned to the steady rhythm, will continue to move even after hitting ground.

"Oh, oh, I can't stop, hold me Arjun," she screams, as she steps off the treadmill, and collides into the trainer, who, well aware of impending doom, is hastily retreating from the oncoming 160-pound, well-fed, feminine missile. Too late, too sweet. Bust rams into chest. His heart skips a beat. Strong arms encircle her ample shoulders, breaking her fall, and forestalling his.

She wants him to hold her, just a little longer, for being so close to this strong man feels so good. He feels likewise, and guilty. Life would be simpler if women were not so desirable. He wants to let go, yet holds on, unwilling to end the romantic interlude.

"Mmmmm." Neelam buries her face into his chest. "Please madam, let me go,." Arjun pleads weakly. She responds by holding him closer, an impossible feat under the circumstances.

"Well," she says philosophically, overcoming the urge within and taking a firm step back. "Let's break right here. If we continue, it will lead to a different form of exercise."

* * *

The exercise of tracking a missing person, as a good police officer will acknowledge, is both art and science. Art because the tracker often has to rely on intuition and play a hunch. Science because the police department has set down procedures that help zero in on the quarry. The activity is often elaborate, painstaking, and driven more by perspiration than inspiration. Elimination of possibilities is the key and perseverance the sine qua non.

The first and crucial step is to find the center, the core around which the missing person's life revolves. From within emerge threads, and then a tapestry, yielding clues to the mystery.

In the case of the chiffon girl, the core was her neighbourhood, people and places she would visit or frequent. The corner shop, where as an eight or ten-year-old, she would have been dispatched on errands during long, hot summers – to fetch betel nuts for her grandfather, a tin of prickly heat powder for sweltering daddy, and chunks of ice to dunk into mother's sherbet. The local lending library where she borrowed her first Enid Blyton, swooned over Mills & Boon or made shy eye contact with the neighbourhood Adonis. The physician down the street who cured her aches, pains and flu. The place of worship where her mother faithfully prayed for the well being of the family, specially the little angel who came in last.

The diligent Inspector Kumaravel began his pursuit in full earnest, breathing down a cold trail at Trustpakkam, where the girl first lived, where Arjun's mind was still in orbit. As he had expected, the results were nothing much to write home about. Yet his job was to eliminate, turn every stone, micro-examine every possibility.

From Trustpakkam, he shifted focus to the apartment complex on D'Silva Road, near Devaki Hospital. The flat the girl and her husband had rented had changed hands three times in 15 years. The secretary of the complex had records dating from its inception, but the likely owner during the time of the girl's tenancy, had been dead and gone for 15 years. The local post office had no record of a forwarding address of the flat at any point in 20 years.

The grocery store owner opposite the complex had raised his eyebrows when the inspector queried him, and then explained he had bought the shop recently, and the previous owner had settled in a remote village in Tirunelveli district. There were no leads at the milk vending booth, laundry or garage mechanic down the road, either. The family had apparently stayed for over a year but forged no bonds in the neighbourhood. Must have been a temporary abode while a home elsewhere was being built or remodeled, reflected the inspector, as he pondered over an uninspiring cup of coffee at a rickety café on adjacent Oliver Road. He was not perturbed; he had solved tougher puzzles. His trained mind ticked off the remaining places where the trail could be resumed: Land records at the office of the deputy registrar, which would reflect sale or purchase or property. Not possible, without a name. Wait, the girl must have pursued a hobby – Carnatic music, piano lessons, embroidery... what was that called... crochet!

He returned next day and pursued every teacher of art and craft in the vicinity. Patience and hard work paid off, leading him to her one-time music teacher.

"I think her name is Rasika, or that's what everyone called her. But that was not her full name though. She told me her name had something to do with music, but these girls, they never complete what they start saying..."

The second finger of his right hand was busy as he spoke, applying in swift strokes white lime on a glistening betel leaf. He folded the leaf, tore out the stem, and deftly tucked it into his mouth. Next, the vital step in the ritual, a plug of rose-scented tobacco culled out from a tin and plugged aside the back teeth.

"As I was saying, Rasika is what I called her. It's been so long, even if she had told me her full name, I can't remember."

* * *

A name, rather a half name, was all the indefatigable Inspector Kumaravel had at the end of three days in the field. They must have had a bank account, the persistent investigator said to himself as he scoured the records of the three nationalised banks in the vicinity. He prayed they had a joint account, and he hoped he would find the name "Rasika" in the ledger. No such luck. Logic, not luck is the key, he chided himself, as he contemplated the next likely trail. If elimination was the key, it was also turning out to be his nemesis, for he was on the verge of eliminating every possibility. Should he admit defeat and get on with his work? Would it matter to Arjun if the girl were not found? There must have been an underlying reason why Arjun wanted to meet her. Why, after 20 years? Halt... he had been proceeding too long on the "how."

Turn to the "why," think out of the box. Retrace the events narrated by Arjun. A garden restaurant on Cathedral Road on a cool January evening. Boy acts fresh with a girl, Arjun enters the scene, rebuffs the boy. The girl and Arjun exit. The rebuked boy who was ticked off by Arjun would have got in touch with the girl, either to apologize or avenge. Find the boy, he could find the girl. Starting point Woodys. Even if the lead turned out cold, even if she could not be found, there was always a pacifier: Piping hot filter coffee.

* * *

She had to be found. I decided to take another shot on my own, although I had entrusted the assignment to Inspector Kumaravel. While he had promised to help, and referred me on to his junior officer who took down the details, I gathered from him and the buzz around the control room that the team was busy preparing for a critical, sensitive assignment: the arrest of a former union minister who had been accused of corruption during a tenure in the petroleum ministry. Apparently, the police expected a backlash from his political followers in the State and were preparing for the eventuality with a firm strategy.

I asked the cabbie to take me to the apartment complex again. Rather than ask the residents, I approached the nearest provision store. The Madras housewife has a habit of ordering her monthly consumables from the same outlet, month after month, and a pattern once set is rarely broken.

The typical shopkeeper in Madras will not talk, unless you buy something from him. Every day, since numerous people stop by, asking for an address, directions, or the nearest phone booth, he considers such queries a waste of his trading time. I made a tactical purchase of provisions, which would last a family an entire month. I chatted him up

67

while he was ordering his boy to pack this and that for me. I let drop casually that I had moved recently into the neighbourhood, but had been here once many years ago at the complex opposite, to visit a friend, and even pointed out the particular apartment, or flat as they say here, to him. "Oh, Mr. Pillai's flat, you know him is it…." Not Pillai. I knew the previous occupant. You knew them too? The family who lived there had two children. Remember them?"

"Don't know, Ayya, I just bought this shop two years ago, from my cousin."

The boy picked up the packets and brought them to the taxi. Jambu was amused to see the purchases, as he knew I had no use for them, but he managed to keep a straight face. I did not share his amusement, because over 2000 rupees worth of provisions – oil, rice, detergent, talcum powder, toothpaste, jar of honey, biscuits, pulses, sugar and butter - had not yielded a single clue.

I gave the boy a 20-rupee tip, not realising it was overly generous by Indian standards. The boy's face lit up. "Saar, I can find out where that family lives," he spoke suddenly, very much wanting to repay my generosity. "My sister used to work as their maid when they were here. I will get the address for you tomorrow. She is not at home now." Some light, at last. I asked Jambu to meet the boy in the morning and collect the vital information before reaching the hotel. And as we left the area, I asked him to take my purchases home. He said he would adjust it against the fare for the days I hired him, but I would not have it. For the strange things I do, why should he lose hard cash?

It was past nine o'clock. I did not feel like going back to the hotel and eating there. Five-star food is fine for the first and second meals, after that the rich ingredients and large portions tend to put you off. "Jambu, let's go to T. Nagar, Geeta Bhavan, near Panagal Park."

I had two reasons to go to that part of city. Food was one.

Two years after I relocated to the United States, my mother had spent three months with me in Colorado. While the fresh cool mountain air is invigorating to the healthy, it often aggravated her asthma. She also found it difficult to stay at home alone the whole day, waiting for me to return from work. I was unhappy to see her leave, and she to go.

68

When news reached of her sudden death in India, I was devastated. I had come to the U.S.A on a H-1 visa and had renewed it three times over eight years. A few months before her death, I had finally been sponsored as an immigrant by my organization. Much as I ached to go, I did not make the trip to her funeral.

In the late 1980s, if you were outside the United States and your application for immigration was pending, chances were you would have to wait it out while the process was completed. Even if I had been free to travel, I would have never reached Madras in time for the funeral, for the journey with stopovers took more than a day. To perform the remaining last rites, I had to make a choice between being practical and emotional: Do my duty as an only son, and then face the consular officer in Madras for my return visa, or avoid the trip and retain her memories. I had been practical.

Inspector Kumaravel, more a family member than a colleague in the force, had conducted all the ceremonies. A month after her passing, Kumaravel had sent me a trunk containing her personal effects. Browsing through the contents one Sunday morning, I found an array of items she had collected and preserved from childhood. Her mother's photo taken at a family function. The old lady was standing at one corner, at what must have been a valaikappu ceremony, where the mother-to-be is decked with bangles on her wrists, and the priests chant mantras for the well being of the progeny. I knew why my grandmother had stayed in the background: Because of taboo. Because she was a widow, who would not be wanted in the forefront during an auspicious ceremony.

I also found a Kalki Deepavali Malar, an annual special issue from the renowned publication house to commemorate the festival of lights, and oft preserved as a collector's item. There were various other family photographs and two mementos from her early and only education: a transfer certificate from her secondary, certifying that she had passed the Std. 9 exams successfully. The other, a book of poems, a carryover from her primary days, possibly Std. 2 or 3. It was tattered, as you would expect, and there were pages missing. What intrigued me was a note she had written on a particular page, containing just one stanza of a poem. The next page which would have contained the remaining stanzas had fallen out, somewhere, sometime, during the last half century.

This is the verse I found:

In the heart of a seed,

Buried deep, oh, so deep

A dear little plant

Lay fast asleep

And the note, scribbled on the bottom left hand corner, said:

"Give me hope, give me faith, and give me a good husband whom I can love till my very end... Give me a child who will give other children what I do not have. Marakatham, April 15, 1945. "

This was written when she had been forced to leave school for monetary reasons. I often wondered what the rest of the stanzas said, and why this verse had prompted her to write the note of hope.

She was from a humble background, born to lower middle class parents. Her father had died early, and she had grown up in the care of a helpful but poor uncle. He had tried to send her to school, but she said she had to stop at the 9th standard, and help him for many years in his catering business. My father, then a young police officer, had placed an order with her uncle for a passing-out parade, and that's how he met her, took an instant liking to her, and soon they were married.

I had always wanted to visit the school where she studied. After a simple meal served on a banana leaf at Geeta Bhavan, I gave the address to Jambu. We found it in a few minutes, a government school, tucked away in West Mambalam, near the railway track. The street was deserted, the school gates had just a bolt one could slide open. The office was locked, the classroom doors just shut. There seemed to be no watchman, probably because the brick and mortar held nothing to protect.

I told Jambu to wait at the end of the street, pushed open the gate and entered the compound, treading the ground that had touched my mother's feet 50 years ago. I wanted to wander around, but my feet felt

70

like lead, anchored to the emotions that the soil had stored for 50 years. I could picture a fatherless child, sent by a poor mother to live with a relative of meagre means. Stepping in everyday, into the school where I now stood. Wearing worn-out clothes, carrying a patched satchel, and little hope for the future. No Enid Blyton for her. No outings with friends, no picnics, dainty frocks, or fancy footwear.

A lump formed in my throat. I leaned against the wall, eyes closed, letting the tears flow. Tears, not because my mother was no more. Because she missed out on what a child should have most: a happy childhood.

No one heard me sob; perhaps my mother would. When I opened my eyes, Jambu was standing in front of me. His wrist clasped mine. His native intelligence told him what I had not. "Come Thambi, let us go. Don't hang on to the past. Look at the future."

I could not, because for me, the future could never beckon, the way the past did. I longed to retrace my mother's steps, relive her early years through ESP, planchette, or Serialism, the psychic experience of going back in time. I craved at that moment for divine grace, for His loving hands to gently rock the cradle of my past, to transport me back in time, to a past I was not part of, but buried deep in my gene.

* * *

CHAPTER FIVE

Time sealed her away, yet she is dwelling still,

like one who sleeps in timelessness,

at the bottom of the timeless sea

Deep in the heart of Mylapore, in a bustling market area called Madaveethi, on the perimeter of Kapali temple, and near the temple tank called Chitrakulam, there exists to this day, a special shop that sells a food item that completes the menu in a typical South Indian home: Appalam, or papad as North Indians would term it. Great with sambar, best with rasam, terrific with Vengaya vatrakkulambu, on Sunday mornings. Consumed with a culinary fervor and crackling sounds, as the fried paper-thin preparation disintegrates, and gets quickly mixed with rice and rasam – the trick is to get through before it gets too soggy, just after it becomes less brittle.

While the shop is called Ambi's Appalam, and while appalams will always be its core product, the outlet sells much more. Vadaams, a thicker and smaller version of the appalam, chips made of banana and potato, mango and lime pickle, various condiments that are essential for a South Indian home, for cooking and ceremonies, and the delicious eatable that has drawn generations to the store – peanut balls, made of select raw peanuts, and rolled golf-ball size using sticky, molten jaggery syrup for bonding and taste.

Back to the appalam. Each appalam is hand made. From a paste of ground and cooked rice (or pulse if it has to be ulundu appalam), first gathered into balls and rolled out into an almost perfect circle, into the size of a 85 rpm record that in another era was played on the gramaphone. The appalams are then sun dried, on a terrace.

The rolling out of the appalams is with a nine pin on a circular marble slab, by a band of young, middle aged or old women, who have no other means of livelihood, hailing from lower middle class, hovering on a thin line between poverty and subsistence. Women like Marakatham. All of 17 years, committed to creating the perfect, even-thickness appalams for her uncle who was sub-contracted by the city's leading stores.

72

As she sat at the corner of the terrace, armed with a stick to ward off roving birds and shielded by a black umbrella, she wondered what the future had in store for her. Her past had never held promise. The future always held hope, because it continued to beckon, and one day she hoped to arrive where she wanted to belong, in a happy, secure world with a loving husband and caring children.

Driving away a daring crow, stealing glances at the pages of the Deepavali Malar in her hand, her thoughts wandered to her early days... her father who died young, in a road accident while cycling home from work. She remembered the owner of the car parts manufacturing company he worked for, coming home for condolence, leaving an envelope behind, containing cash far beyond his entitlement, for his service had been short. She remembered the kind man because he had an unusual practice. He employed over 200 workmen in his factory; and every working day, one family would be invited to have lunch with the owner in his room, and that covered the rolls, from vice president to welder and fitter. He did it right through the year, and they had got their turn towards the end of her father's first and only year in service. She remembered the lunch served in bright stainless steel plates, the owner's genuine interest in their life, his little hug when she said thank you. There were good people on earth.

Much as she did not want to, she remembered her father's death ceremony too... rice in his mouth just before his brother lit the funeral pyre. Rice balls on a banana leaf during his srardha ceremony, symbolically placed as food for the departed soul. Little to eat for those he left behind.

Her mother working as a cook in a well-to-do household, bringing home leftovers and excess rice that would not be carried over to the next day. Buttermilk, rice and lime pickle in the night. Sweets from the Lala shop during Deepavali. Bun-butter-jam from the street corner bakery on Sunday mornings. Fifteen rupees to the landlord for rent. One anna for bright, pink cotton candy. Always short of money for school fees.

Her uncle visiting them one evening, suggesting Marakatham move to his house, to help him in his appalam business. Grinding rice for the old ladies he employed, cooking the powder in large utensils, over firewood. Packing the end product in lots of 50 and 100. Uncle expanding into contract catering for functions.

73

Her mother's death from a cholera epidemic. Random thoughts - of a difficult childhood, uncertain adolescence.

* * *

Decades later in time, Marakatham's DNA was thinking of her. While driving to Sowcarpet, to the street where her husband had spent his fiery last minutes. I wondered as we drove in, whether the language activists of a quarter century ago looked back at their violent days with pride or shame. The nameboards they had smeared with tar had sprung back, but the tilak on my mother's forehead never did return.

Some parts of Madras never change. Especially North Madras. I did not see a single multi-storey building. Most of the houses had been constructed on a half ground or less of land, like the town houses in the USA or the row houses one finds in suburban Bombay. The house I was heading for was easy to spot, simply because it was the only structure with land around, with a driveway plus a garage. Just outside the house, between the gate and the road, was a leafy tree, bestowing shade on the quaint bungalow.

The Marwari lady had died the previous year, the son told me, after I refreshed his memory about the incident 25 years earlier. I remember him being nervous when we had first met. He was relaxed now, possibly because he knew that it was very unlikely that an investigation was on. I asked him if he remembered me, and the insurance man who had accompanied me.

"What insurance man? He was a policeman no?"

"No, he was my father's insurance agent. He was helping us settle the claim."

"*Arrey, yaar,* what nonsense. People can call themselves what they want, but we know. We have been having shops in this area for 60 years. Every time we see a customer, we know what kind of person he is. Whether he will cause trouble, we can give him credit or not, whether he will make false complaint about the product, everything we know."

Keeping the charade going more than two decades later was pointless. So, I asked him how he knew. "He was wearing brown, polished shoes.

That's the problem with most policemen. They will change clothes, put on cap, change name, but shoes they won't. Even after retirement, they wear those shoes. I spotted him the moment he walked in."

I wondered how often in investigations such die-hard habits gave a policeman away. In any case, if the Marwaris had equivocated, then there was a truth lurking elsewhere. I explained to the Marwari, Gupta was his name, that I wanted to know about the killer as a matter of personal interest.

"Promise me, you won't drag me to court and I will tell you."

"I promise, Mr. Gupta. I want this information for my own peace of mind. Not for filing a case. If you want, I will give you a written undertaking."

Gupta smiled, wryly, and there was a calm in his eyes I had not seen before. "Dost, I do not want your written promise. For us in business, the word is more than enough. We deal in thousands of rupees, only based on what a man says. And we deal only with people who mean what they say.

"You are one of them… I can say that from your eyes, and from the fact you have pursued the same goal after 25 years."

Gupta told me what I had always suspected. That someone who worked in their household had committed the crime. He gave me an address on a piece of paper. Looking at it, I was struck by the irony. My quarry lived close to the sanctum – of one of the Seven Apostles of Christ.

***

St. Thomas Mount. If you are landing at Madras during daylight, it is impossible to miss the hillock on the far side of the airport. At night, all you can glimpse is the twinkling red light on the peak. I had a clear terrestrial view of the little mountain as we skirted cycles and rickshaws on the narrow lanes at the foothills. Jambu was finding the address, leaning out of the window and asking for directions from tea stalls, mango sellers and a watch repairer. He finally parked at a dead end, on the blind side of the airport.

"Saar, that is the house. You have to walk up the slope. I will wait here."

Not just the slope, but I had to traverse stones, a rivulet of drainage and a brood of chicks to reach the home. A 20-something young man opened the door. Now, I do not look like a policeman, but my build is akin to the fit IPS officers you encounter in the force. My melancholy eyes are at times mistaken for the steel-like pair you find in those who hunt down dacoits and extract the truth from serial killers. The young man took one step back, regained composure, and asked in a neutral, non-offensive tone:

"Whom do you want, sir?"

"I am looking for Arumugam."

"He is not here. Gone to his native place. Back next month only." A low cough emanated from the next room, and quickly developed into a staccato sound.

"And he left his cough behind. Look, tell him I am not from the police. I have not come to collect any debts. I am from America. Mr. Gupta from Sowcarpet sent me here."

He was still defensive but the fear had lessened. He opened the door fully and asked me to come in. "Father, someone to meet you."

We grow up indoctrinated by this theory of crime and punishment, imbibed from the Panchatantra tales, fables, folklore and occasionally real life incidents. Arumugam, the man who set fire to my father seemed in good shape. He said he had worked for the Guptas for just a year, when he was drawn into the language agitation movement. They had promised him a municipal councillor's seat if he served faithfully. During the first three months he had just tarred name boards and stoned public places, then as the movement grew violent, and as some of his co-agitators were arrested, he started believing that if he struck back with a daring act, he would be glorified as a hero. On the fateful day, Arumugam had been in the forefront of the demonstration at Sowcarpet when my father's convoy had attempted to quell the riot that had broken out. When four demonstrators fell to his bullets, Arumugam had been goaded into torching the fearless inspector. He had rushed into his employer's compound, picked up a burning log of wood from the kitchen fire, covered his face with a bright red veil from the clothesline, and jumped over the short wall on to the street.

Fearing being apprehended by the police, he had left the next day for Delhi. He secured a job as driver with a South Indian family in RK Puram, where he served for over 25 years. He said the act of torching the policemen had haunted him for the rest of his life. No solace for me. I had just one father.

The man had committed third degree murder, yet here he was a quarter century later, untouched by the long arm of the law. Suddenly, I was tired of my mission, my misplaced goals, and the sheer injustice of it all. I did not want to stay any longer. The last thing I heard as I headed for the taxi was the sound of a grown man crying.

As we drove around the road that lapped at the foothills, Jambu said, "Saar, you know those people in that house?" It seemed Jambu wanted to talk. I did not wish to. "No, I don't know them," I said curtly.

He paid no heed to my snapping at him. "I was having tea nearby saar. That man Arumugam in the house – he also a driver. He worked in Delhi. The tea stall fellow says Arumugam had a daughter. Took her to Haridwar to bathe in Ganga river. She lost her grip on the chains they fix on the bank for pilgrims. The father try to hold her, but he had sudden shooting pain in his hand. Missed holding her. The current swept her away. Many, many, years ago."

In the Lord's ledger book, every debit has a credit. In His calendar, time is not reckoned by clock, because our entire lifetime is in His hands. We may commit a crime, and escape notice. We like to believe the world has forgotten forever. The truth is, the Lord has a crystal clear memory.

Somewhere atop the Mount, a bell tolled, reminding me of His other side: Merciless in spirit, matchless in anger, boundless in penalty. On Judgement Day, Arumugam, who had lived by the sword, did not die by it. Worse still, he watched a loved one die.

* * *

"He may not live beyond a few days, it's a miracle that he has survived this long, something is holding him…"

77

Place: Korattur, an hour from Madras. Location: The living room of retired constable Mathivanan, in the first floor apartment of a police housing complex. Date: Day four of my sojourn in Madras. Time: Noon. I remained standing while the woman accompanied the physician to the ground floor.

I had reached Korattur by bus from Madras. Jambu had taken the day off, professing personal work. I did not ask him what his preoccupation was. Live too long in the United States and you cannot see beyond your nose.

An auto in its last days took me from the town bus stand to the address given by Inspector Kumaravel. He said Mathivanan had retired a few years earlier, and now lived with his son and daughter-in-law in Korattur. Being a native himself, he had given me precise directions to the residence, so the auto fellow had no chance of making an extra buck that morning. I tipped him five rupees anyway. He thanked me profusely and offered to wait for half hour.

"I am Inspector Kumaramangalam's son," I announced when the daughter returned to the apartment.

"Sorry, I could not even ask who you are, or ask you to sit down. We are so worried about father that we tend to forget even normal courtesies. He has been suffering from bronchitis for the last few years and the last two weeks have been very bad. We are hoping he will get better but I don't know... his condition has been worsening since morning." Tamil in rural areas is spoken fast and at a stretch, I knew, but this woman's delivery was rapid. "My father used to talk so much about your father. I will tell him Ayya's son has come, he will be pleased to see you, but give me a minute, first I will ensure he takes his medicine."

Mathivanan, to term it right, was not pleased to see me, but for some reason a wave of relief seemed to cross his face as I sat next to his bed and leaned forward to hear him speak. "I never met your mother after that morning thirty years ago. I did not have the heart to see her. Your father's death has always weighed on my heart. I wish he had listened to me, he should never have gone alone to the police station."

"I agree with you. But you know that is the only way he would have acted. But what happened to the gathering... from what I know, the student leader had cleared the way, and had promised his safety in case he came unarmed."

"You are talking about Guna I suppose. He was a good man. He believed truly that the agitation had a cause, and that he was fighting for preserving the Tamil language. But he did not realize vested interests had their own agenda, and would not allow a peaceful protest to remain peaceful. There was also another side to it. With Inspector Venkatesh as hostage, there was a plan among the die hards to make demands to the government, failing which they would execute him. Guna, being only in his second year of college, did not know all this. So, when he allowed your father to walk through, there was an altercation between him and the militant group. In the process, he was attacked and a head injury from a stone thrown at him, rendered him unconscious. When he fell, the students loyal to him were chased away and the hard core group took over."

"You are many years older to me, and I should not ask you this. But you and the other policemen, if you had started shooting at the mob, would you have managed to disperse them? I know you were outnumbered but had you opened fire, there was a chance of scattering them."

Almost for a minute, he did not answer. "We had to decide between courage and logic," he said presently. "As you know, there were over 3000 protesters – we could have taken maybe twenty lives and then the irate mob would have overpowered us. Inspector Ilango, the second in command, ordered us to turn back. I was the only person who did not want to. I had to obey because I had to drive the jeep. The reason I did not want to leave, I will tell you, not because I am brave, not because I am good policeman, but because I knew that one day I would have to answer you. I was hoping I would die before that, but in my last days you have come. Forgive me for what I did not do, only then can I die in peace."

"I am not angry with you. You had no choice because of the situation. Had you stayed on, perhaps you would not be alive to tell me this story. One question before I leave: Is Guna till in Madras?"

"Very much. Not very easy to meet him though. He is the Law

Minister for the State of Tamil Nadu. Kumaravel knows him well."

* * *

"There are three policemen on duty in the morning. One is posted at the security booth at the gate, another drops the children to school and attends to domestic errands. The third loiters in the porchway keeping an eye on visitors. The best time to meet Guna, sorry, the Hon'ble Minister Thiru Gunasekaran, is in the morning, when he returns from his walk. Don't tell him I said that. He is back by seven, there are no cronies around at this time, and the rush of visitors would not have started. He normally likes to spend a quiet half hour with his wife on the veranda, drinking coffee and enjoying the only cigarette she allows, but this week she has gone to her mother's place. I suspect he will be eager for company... although you are not what he would bargain for."

To meet the Law Minister at seven, I would have to miss my run and stretches. He lived on Greenways Road, the area where most ministers of the Govt. of Tamil Nadu are put up, in a mid size bungalow set amid greenery, next to the abode of a Justice of the High Court. A driveway stretched for over 150 metres from the road to his residence, reflecting a colonial past and perks of modern day office. I had risen early as usual, and kicked off the run at five thirty... Chola to Gandhi statue, left there, straight up to Vivekananda House, Anna Square and the Iron Bridge, turnaround at the War Memorial and straight down like an arrow to Santhome Church and St Bede's school, then Foreshore Estate, Music College, Sathya Studio intersection and on to Greenways Road, and a warm down thereafter. Not wanting to seek admission dripping in sweat, I had tied a light sweat shirt around my waist and had changed discreetly behind a broad tree trunk.

Vettri, Vettrivendhan, I remembered the full name. On duty till 730. "Vanakkam Vettrivendan, ACP aiya sent me. ACP Kumaravel. I have come to meet Mr. Gunasekaran."

References work the world over. His sombre face brightened and the crease on his brow, caused by the appearance of a brawny six footer in non political attire, softened. "Yes, he called me last night. Halt, while I report to the honourable minister. Whom should I say has come?"

My name would have no meaning. "Please tell him the son of

80

Inspector Kumaramangalam is here to meet him. I just want five minutes of his time." The constable picked up the intercom and spoke to someone inside, possibly the minister himself as the secretaries would not be present at this time.

"I am sorry sir, "the constable said, replacing the receiver with all the fizz out of him. "He says please submit a petition to his personal secretary at Government Secretariat, in case there is something you need. He says he does not recall a Kumaramangalam nor has anyone spoken to him about you."

Kumaravel had specifically declined from speaking to the minister. He said I should get the meeting on my own steam. He was also not sure whether it would be "politically correct" to introduce me into the scene, the subject of the anti-Hindi agitation being passé in the present. He had spoken to the security staff to ensure I crossed the first hurdle and the rest was up to me.

"I will wait here... can you send this to him, it might help." The photocopy of a newspaper report of the 1960s, chronicling the death of my father, with a box item on the student leader who had led the protest. Slightly wet with sweat, but it should do.

* * *

The coffee was strong but a little watery. There was no sugar on the table, only a substitute called Equal, which I declined and set forth on the bitter concoction instead. Policeman No. 2 had ushered me in, I had been welcomed with a warm hug, and indicated to sit down, but not a word had been spoken from the time we were seated. The minister was inhaling deep on his cigarette, his coffee growing cold on the side table.

"We were all fighting for a cause then. It seemed the most important goal in our life," his voice broke the morning silence. He was looking away from me, at the road, the trees and vehicles passing by.

"We did not have an idea or inkling of the era ahead. A time when borders, state and international, would have no meaning, and business, trade and commerce would move people seamlessly from place to place, when knowledge of languages would be an advantage.

"Hindi, we believed, was an indirect form of invasion, by the North on the South. I was young then, and at that impressionable age, the cause seemed worth fighting for. As a student leader, I lead from the front... we burnt the books of those who chose Hindi as a second language in pre university. We marched to All India Radio when its name was changed to Akashvani. We submitted a petition against broadcast of Hindi news in Tamilnadu, samachar it was called. We tore down film banners in theatres which screened Hindi films. One thing for sure, in the protests I organized, the question of injuring anyone did not arise. Yet, since I was gaining name and fame as a leader, I was invited to bring students from my college and three others to the massive protest organized in Sowcarpet. It was all organized in secret overnight. When our group joined the others, I realized that the rally included not just politicians part of the language agitation but several goondas who were known to cause trouble.

"When your father arrived on the scene, the crowd wanted to attack him. They were fully charged and were bolstered by the fact that the posse was outnumbered. I did not want bloodshed, I talked them into allowing your father to pass through and rescue the other inspector from the police station. I still can't forget the bold manner in which he dropped his gun."

"When my father returned with Inspector Venkatesh you were lying unconscious. What happened in those few minutes?"

"One of the goondas came to me and patted me on the shoulder. I was surprised. He said my masterplan was working... and they would fulfill it. I probed him and he told me something that curdled my blood. He said I had successfully tricked the inspector into entering the police station, we would have two hostages. If the government refused our demands, then as per my plan they would burn down the structure. I was aghast because it was obvious that people were playing games, using my name for their motives. I refuted his statement and called my supporters to take charge of the situation. While we were arguing, your father had exited the police station and was walking towards the mob. I pleaded with the ruffians not to harm the inspectors, stressing that men of valour should be given due respect. I was attacked at that point and as I was losing consciousness, I could hear the argument continuing with my supporters whether to let the policemen leave the area. That is why your father had time to reach the jeep. The sight of them leaving, infuriated the goondas for it meant that they were being ignored. They prodded the gathering to attack the jeep. You know the rest."

I am not one given to arguments. I also believe that a point well stated is to be accepted. In a way, the matrix of my father's death was almost falling in place. I had been to the spot where he breathed his last, watched his killer struggling for reprieve, understood the predicament of his driver, and now I had confronted the man whom I believe is indirectly responsible for his death, for if youngsters like him had perceived the ugly side of the protests, people like my father would have lived from bud to blossom. I had no further questions. I thanked him for meeting me without a proper appointment and for explaining the circumstances of the tragedy.

"Come, I will walk down with you to the gate. You are a rare visitor in my world. Most people who come here ask for a favour or want to trade favours for money. I keep them at bay. They make sure I am not popular in political circles. Our leader is ailing, they know I am next in line but are organizing a secret memorandum to ensure that Thenappan, the current minister for revenue, succeeds in case our leader relinquishes office due to ill health. His portfolio is quite appropriate, except that all the revenue he generates is for himself. It is a surprise he is not behind bars yet. Let's leave all that, the world I live in is different, rules don't apply. Tell me if there is anything I can do for you while you are in Madras. By the way, you look like a policeman. If you were younger I would have recommended you to the force. Did it ever cross your mind?"

"I was very young when my father died. When I grew up my mother told me that a month after my father's death, the inspector general of police, Mr. Dhairiyam, had passed an order that if I were ever to opt for police service when I grew up, I should be given preference on compassionate grounds, subject to prevailing tests of merit. I was keen, but my mother would not allow it. You can guess why."

The minister waited patiently while I entered the security booth and collected my wet t-shirt. I shook hands with him and was about to turnaround and leave, when on an impulse, he hugged me. "My heart has always been heavy from that day," he said suddenly, fighting back tears. "His death brought home the other side of politics. When I opened my eyes in hospital that evening, I took a pledge... that I would always stay away from such moves to gain power. That I would never ever resort to violence or allow people around me to use it as a tool. That is why it has taken me this long to become a minister.

"I learnt something from your father. That it is more important to save another than to save yourself... you know that when he was hiding in a corner in the ice factory, the other policeman was discovered and led away. Had you father chosen to remain silent, he would have lived, but such a selfish act would have tortured him for the rest of his life. A month after his death, as a mark of my learning, I did something as a tribute to the departed soul.

"I planted a tree, just outside the bungalow where he breathed his last. In its strong roots, and the leaves that offer shade, his memory lives forever."

* * *

Never before had he felt so alive. His neck emanated a sweet sensation for days after Neelam's touch. She was all he could think of the next few days. Their relationship had taken a new turn. From just a friendly neighbour, she had become a close friend, not by words but by action. In a way, he was proud of the attention she gave him. He felt a bond with her that he had never known earlier with a woman.

Having got this close mentally and physically, he felt he could discuss any subject with Neelam, or more precisely the unfulfilled yearnings that gnawed at his mind: He wished to amend his relationship with his cousin. He longed to restore the association with the girl at the garden restaurant. He craved to look into the eyes that witnessed his father's death. He very much wanted to tread the ground of his mother's childhood. He wanted the past back.

He got his chance to revisit a page of the past, strangely enough, the same week. He woke up on Tuesday to find a note from Neelam slipped under the door. She had left overnight for South Africa to visit her father-in-law who had suffered a heart attack. As he was reading the note, appreciating her empathy, and wishing she had returned his spare key, which was with her for emergencies, the phone rang. It was his Uncle from Colby, Kansas, local head honcho of Wal-Mart, one of the nation's largest and most successful retail stores founded by Sam Walton. His cousin Nirupama was landing at Kansas City and reaching Colby on Friday night, after many long years. Would he like to visit them and spend the weekend at their home... Uncle's wife was in India, and he said he would appreciate some company to take care of Nirupama during the three days she would spend with him. Normally, he would have declined, but now was the time to resurrect and correct. He promised to drive in Saturday morning and return Sunday evening. A surprised and pleased uncle gave him the directions and rang off.

He was excited. He pulled out the Rand McNally from his desk and surveyed the route. Colby, Kansas, was about 250 miles, may be 4 hrs plus, under 4 if there was no snow. On Friday, he would fill up gas, check lubes, tire pressure and maybe buy a welcome gift for the reunion.

Like the sands in the hourglass are the days of our lives... moving like the particles set to the steady rhythm of the cosmic clock. People enter at some part of the cycle, exit and return in another era, like Nirupama would, 7212 days later. Where did he see her last? At the edge of the tarmac, Madras airport.

He packed carefully on Friday night. His best winter wear went in first. He put in a tie, his favourite navy blue jacket and light gray slacks, just in case uncle decided to take them out on Saturday night. He had bought her a hand held blender with a 220 volts adapter and gift-wrapped it.

His first choice was a cosmetics set, complete with lip-gloss, rouge packs and a hand held mirror, but it didn't seem the right gift from a bachelor to a married woman. The gesture was important, not the product, he had noted, unaware of the events that would unfold the next day. He placed the gift carefully in the side pouch of his travel bag. Something was missing – his survival kit. In went track bottoms and top, shoes, socks, and a pullover plus woolen cap, for it would be sub zero temperature with a high wind chill factor when he ran on Sunday morning.

He did not jog on Saturday morning. He woke up at 5 a.m. was ready by 5.30. Leisure stretches in the living room for 10 minutes, to tone up muscles and loosen joints ahead of the drive. He served himself a portion of cottage cheese, and washed it down with chilled Minutemaid. Close, smooth shave, generous splash of Aramis. Blue jeans, checked flannel shirt, cardigan, travelbag in hand, elevator down to the car park. He warmed up the engine for two minutes, eyes closed, savouring the silence of the morning, and the cold, clean air of Boulder, Colorado. Random thoughts of Neelam, Nirupama and... the nameless girl, forever young in his heart. She would be older now, but he wanted her as she was. He wanted her the way he left her at Mandaveli, Madras, India, 20 years ago, slender and young, but he knew she would have married, spawned children, and dedicated herself to family life, as a loving mother and caring wife.

* * *

He drove out of Boulder on US 36, on to Interstate 76 towards Denver, switched to I-270 and ultimately to the highway that would take him non stop eastward for more than 220 miles on I-70 to Colby. As the engine purred on the highway, for once he dwelled on the future: on his meeting with Nirupama. He would bring up, sometime during the weekend, the incident 20 years ago at her house. Even with his limited knowledge of women, he knew they had a tendency to forget occasions when they were in the wrong. If she claimed amnesia, he would gently tell her how hurt he had been, assuring her that he understood she would never have mistrusted him intentionally. He would come back and tell Neelam all about it.

He pulled into a truck stop around 8 a.m. for breakfast. Food was not top of mind today. Light breakfast of scrambled eggs, hash browns, coffee. At 20 minutes past 10, he was parking at uncle's suburban home in Colby, Kansas. There was a Dodge Van in the driveway, and a second car, a Toyota Starlet, in the garage.

To his surprise, Nirupama opened the door. She had gained weight, and looked a mother of two, which he knew from family sources, she was. "Good to see you, Arjun. Come in... Uncle is just tidying up your room. You never write, or keep in touch, not just with me, but the whole family... tell me how you are, and what you have been doing all these years..."

Uncle joined them shortly. For a man who shunned company, he found that he was actually happy to be in their midst. They were close relatives. It was he who had stayed away. At noon, they had lunch, which Nirupama had cooked, and they spent the afternoon in the study, looking at family albums of two generations, and ending with a screening of slides uncle had shot over the last three decades. He saw wedding pictures of his mother and father, shots of himself as a one-year old, his father as a police cadet and then IPS officer. Memories of life stored and replayed on carousels worldwide, on legendary Kodak film.

He wondered when he would have opportunity for a heart-to-heart talk with Nirupama. As things stood, he would not get a window, unless she was crazy enough to wake up early like him at 5 a.m. come rain, shine or snow.

"Er, you know what Nirupama, why not we go for a walk tomorrow morning?"

"Walk, don't kid me, I am here on holiday. The only walking I do is during my sleep, ha, ha, ha." He was not tactful or experienced enough with women to suggest other ways. That night they had dinner in an Indian restaurant in downtown Colby. The owner obviously knew Uncle well, for they got the best table, strategically placed so you could watch from pole position the Hindi film running on the video wall. Rajesh Khanna, the hero, blinded in the second half of the movie in a car accident, once again meets his love, not knowing it is her and so on and on. A chirpy North Indian woman at the adjacent table was proudly narrating to her son how she and his Daddy had seen the picture, "Mere Jeevan Sathi," first day, first show, years ago in Delhi.

As they were being served warm Gajjar Halwa and ice cream, he had his first opportunity to converse one-to-one with her. The owner wanted to have a word with uncle regarding an alliance for his daughter; the boy was employed in Wal-Mart headquarters. Uncle excused himself, and the waiter carried his dessert to a room adjacent to the kitchen, which served as an office.

For a few minutes, neither spoke. He wondered how to broach the subject. She hoped uncle would return any minute. "It was nice of you to come to the airport to see me off," he began formally. "It is twenty years ago, but I can still remember you, you were wearing a pink colored salwar kameez, right?"

"Aiyo!, how can I remember, I must have come because Mom would have asked me to. I can look back maybe till last year, the earlier times seem very vague now." What she was trying to convey, he realized, was I don't want to remember, because you are not important to me. In case you want to explain the incident, I am not interested.

It struck him then how much of a surface person she was. It was not that she was hollow and false. She was just one of those who had no empathy, who did not care enough to change a view, once a viewpoint was established. She belonged to the category of women whose mind you could never penetrate, simply because there were no hidden emotions to be revealed. He wondered about the man who had married her. Better be a bachelor than wed someone so cold.

He got another chance to be alone with her, a longer duration this time, after they returned home. He was not keen to talk; the sampling at the restaurant was proof enough. It was bitter cold, with the central heating going full blast. Uncle was handing out an electric blanket to Arjun when his beeper shrilled. He quickly rang the store security and identified himself. A fire had broken out in the mall where Wal-Mart was located.

"Be there in 5 minutes. Call Joe and Dennis, will you? We can't have the fire department dousing our stock with water just for fear it will go out of control," he said and hung up.

"Sorry folks, duty calling. I need to rush. There is cocoa powder in the cabinet above the fridge. Nirupama, make some hot chocolate for Arjun and you, watch a Tamil movie if you want to. I will be back, may take a couple of hours."

Nephew secured the door after he left, shot the bolt home, snapped the door chain in place, and turned around. Unlike the condo in Colorado, this was an independent house, with no security except what is offered by the night patrol. He did not know how safe the neighbourhood was, did not want to take chances in a new place, especially when alone with a woman.

His concern was misplaced.

* * *

We got back to Chola from St. Thomas Mount late in the evening. Though I was fulfilling objectives, I was restless, because I had not accomplished my principal mission. I announced a 20-minute break to Jambu, who said he would use it to fill petrol and take a tea break.

"I say, did you get the address of that house from the boy at the grocery. You were supposed to go there today morning, forgot or what?"

Jambu scratched his head. "Sorry saar... Morning no water coming at home. Wife told to catch from corporation tap." Typical local habit. Explain every omission, feel less guilty.

"OK. Do one thing. After you fill gas, go see that boy."

"Gas sir? You want gas for lighter sir, or cooking gas?"

"*Aiyo* Jambu, gas means petrol, in America. Please go to petrol bunk and fill petrol. I don't want any gas, jazz."

I had a quick shower, changed, and put away some fruits and cookies the hotel offers complimentary to guests, followed by coffee. I saw the taxi drive up as I was pacing the lobby. The grocer's boy was sitting in the front, along with a woman. Was this the sister he had mentioned?

Way to go, Jambu! I bounded from lobby to portico.

"Got the address? Where does the family live? How far from here?"

"She knows the street and house sir, correct address and all that these people will not know. I know everything you do is important, so I brought her with me. I promised her 50 rupees, and that you mean no harm to that family. She will show us the place."

The place turned out to be a large bungalow in Anna Nagar West. As I neared the gate, I noticed a young boy wheeling his cycle into the garage. He had a bag on his shoulder. Judging from the time of the day, he must be returning from tuition, an age-old Indian educational concept, which presumes that what's taught in school has to be learnt again in private. All the trappings of a successful husband or a legacy of wealth were evident in the brick and mortar around me. The structure was well maintained, paint in good shape, flowers and shrubs all cared for. There was a half porch that led to the main door. The boy rang the bell. I held my ground at the gate, waiting for the door to open, and wanting to see who would open it. If it were the husband, I would casually walk in. What would I say? "Hello, I helped your wife when a rogue was troubling her 20 years ago, I have come to check if she is all right…" Absolute truth, but he would find it corny. If it were the mother-in-law, the issue would get stickier. If it was her, there was hope.

For once, it was my lucky day. Twenty lonely years later, I saw her again, angel-like in the white porch light. Neelam would have cheered. There was a sereneness about her that set my heart throbbing. Dressed in a blue saree, she was as slim, and as beautiful, with just a tinge of an age line on her face.

"Have you copied all the portions from Rahul, whatever you missed during the last two weeks?" she asked the boy. Intuition caused her to glance toward the entrance. That's when I pushed open the wrought iron gate, and walked into her life once again.

* * *

"Why are you closing the door? You could have gone with uncle," she said nervously.

"It is a fire situation. The area would be cordoned off, and only authorized persons can do anything there. I don't want the hot chocolate, I think I will just go to bed. How about you, shall I put the VHS on for you?"

"Arjun, I think it's better you leave. Why don't you go a bar or something and come back after some time."

Looking back, he was sure what infuriated him was not the suggestion he leave. It was asking him to go to a "bar." Such were the traits of women. They would generalize all men as molesters, alcoholics and womanizers. They would not care enough about a man to know his value systems. Why ascribe a positive trait when you are in possession of a negative. Why give a person a fair chance?

He had no time to dwell on her judgment errors because she was saying something, infuriating him further and proving that times change, people don't. They will cling to their inhibitions, suspicions, fears and foolhardiness.

"Don't mistake me, but you have been a bachelor all these years. I do not know what kind of person you have become."

"What kind of person I have become?" he snapped, repeating her words.

"I can see you have not changed at all. You have changed from bad to worse." His rage did not diminish when he saw her cringing, and close to tears.

"All right, we will do it your way. I am going to my room to change. I will leave the house for a few hours. Until I go out, stay near this door, so that you can escape if you have to."

He dressed fast, and in five minutes, he was at the driveway. The temperature was four degrees below zero.

There was no wind, just a bitter cold that enveloped the roads, trees and his heart. He had his schedule worked out for the next two hours. Something he could always do, come rain, shine, snow, or Nirupama. A good long run in a world of his own.

It was an affluent neighbourhood on the west side of town. He had noticed while driving into the subdivision that it was bounded by a perimeter of road that enclosed the precinct. Smaller roads fed into this main one. He estimated that one outer round would be five miles; three rounds would take him about 2 hours.

Chrono set to 0, woolen cap and mittens tightly in place, three minutes walk down the road, muscle stretches to reassure the surprised joints, two minutes running on the spot... he kicked off with thoughts of the past, summoning a world he wished to return to: Walking up the winding staircase in the middle of the night, snuggling next to his mother, her protective arms drawing him closer. Memories of his father, tall and upright, in police uniform. His mother tucking jasmine flowers in her hair, his father helping her set it right, smiling and placing his hand on her shoulder, his fingers squeezing her shoulder just a little and then relaxing, his mother blushing, turning her face away. Watching his mother sew a button on his tunic, step close and snap the string with her teeth. Father, mother and son watching an English film at Elphinstone. Peach melba ice cream, decked with two tall, slim wafers, at Jaffar's next door.

His nostrils protested against the cold air driving in and out. After the first 15 minutes, he could gradually bring down the rasping of breath to a steady rhythm. Unlike Colorado, the terrain was flat, and mean sea level zero. He felt like an athlete who had trained at high altitude and was now racing in the plains. In 30 minutes, he was in form, relentlessly maintaining his footfall, mind far away on the chiffon clad girl. Strangely, he was thankful to Sudhakar and Nirupama for binding his life with the girl, not physically or geographically, but at an astral level where he could roam free with her.

He grimaced as his thoughts zeroed in on the girl. She would be married now, and that was his life's greatest tragedy. Much as he did not want to, his mind was played out her marriage ceremony, temperature below zero notwithstanding.

The mehendi ceremony on the penultimate day, the bride dressed in a silk saree, decked with jewels, the night that she would have slept thinking of her marriage, and the man who would enter her life the next day. Next morning the build up to the kanyadanam - clear, milk-like feet at the oonjal, the traditional swing wherein the bride and groom are seated, women gathered around singing in chorus. The clock would wear on, leading to the ceremony of a lifetime. The bride emerges attired in the traditional red sari, and is seated on her father's lap. The proud man gives the bride away (oh, stop, please stop, she is mine), the groom ties the thali, the sacred gold string, around the bride's neck, first knot, second, third, the final tightening of the third knot - the closure of hope.

The clasp of a male hand on her slender wrist, shower of rice and blessings from those older, he introduces her to his friends, well wishers, she acknowledges, smiles, relishes her new and lifelong status as a wife.

The "reception" in the evening, the traditional event where invitees throng to wish the newlyweds, the grand dinner at night, and then bidding farewell to guests, friends and relatives. She changes her saree, perhaps a printed silk that wraps tight around her slender waist, and then… thoughts shatter to smithereens, he cannot, will not, visualize further. Mind halts pantomime, returns to where it all started: Her finger on his blood. Lingering a fraction longer.

A patrol car pulls up ahead. Flashing of beacon lights, back to reality and the biting cold.

Nothing is unusual in the United States. The axiom notwithstanding, a man jogging at midnight in winter cannot be termed a common occurrence. A burly cop in his late 50s got out. "Can I see some ID please? Stand still, I need to check your eyes for dope."

He pulled out his driver's license, something you carry in the United States even if you are not driving, and gave it to the officer. "I would appreciate if you sit with me in the car, I need to check you out."

"Officer, I can't stop now, because I am on a two hour run. I can jog round the car while you check out my license."

"You are not a Chico are you? Which part of the world are you from?"

"I am not from Mexico; I am from India," he answered jogging on the spot. In most parts of the United States, Indians are perceived as law abiding, industrious and engaged in legal businesses or tech careers. This perception worked in his favor.

"Go on with your run. But I'll bet my last dollar something's not right at home."

The rest of the run was uneventful. He stopped his chrono at 2 hours, and warmed down with a walk for about 10 minutes, working his way towards the house. Uncle had not returned, Nirupama had not gone to sleep. She was in the living room. The television was reeling off an old Western, but she was looking at the screen vacantly. He could see that she had cried.

"What's wrong? Any call from uncle?"

"He called just now. The fire's under control. He will be back in 15 minutes. Arjun, please. I am sorry Arjun, for what I did. I was thinking back, I realize I reacted the same way in Madras, that day you brought flowers home. You took such insults from me, and even after that you came here to meet me. Will you forgive me, please?"

Damn the English language. It has words like "sorry" and "forgive", which one can use at will. Her words would not assuage his deep hurt or alter his views on women. She had gained clarity only after making the same mistake twice. Meaningless words came to his rescue as well.

"You were right, you know. You just don't know whether I am good or bad. Let us forget all about this, and don't tell uncle I went out in the night."

He left soon after breakfast on Sunday morning. Uncle was too preoccupied with his store to question his professed reason for the early departure. He drove non-stop to Boulder, and entered the condo at 2 p.m., tired, irritable, and hungry. As he was turning the key in his apartment door, it opened from within, and he retreated with a startle.

Neelam: dressed in a housecoat, hair tied in a bun, a mini vac in one hand, mop in another.

"Welcome home, young man. Or from the look of it, angry young man."

"When did you come back? What are you doing here?"

She set the vac and mop down and held her hands out straight, resting them on his shoulders, keeping him at arm's length to study his face. "Come, come, don't take out your hassles on me. Would you like to have a wash, and drop in for some hot soup and food? We can talk after that."

It turned out she did not fly out of the United States. On reaching New York, she had telephoned her husband for an update on his father's condition. He had said that the patient was stable, but the country was not, due to a coup attempt. He had asked her to return to Boulder. She had come home, found Arjun away, had time on her hands, hence decided to clean up his apartment.

He surveyed his home after she left. He kept a reasonably clean house, but never spent time cleaning out the cupboards. Neelam had been through every closet. His ties, pants, shirts and accessories were all neatly folded and in place. The laundry bag was empty. She must have run a load. He found himself relaxing and unwinding as he went around the spotless kitchen, clean living room, and fresh linen in the bedroom. Felt good to have a woman around.

She served him lunch in her apartment. While he was helping her place the plates in the dishwasher, she asked casually, "This is personal, but I am going to ask. That hanky I found in your drawer. You seem to have preserved it for a long, long time. Also, I found some autographed photographs of a woman - looked like an aging actress trying to stay in shape."

Had it been anyone else, he would have been offended at the intrusion. In a way, he was glad she was direct and got to the point. He did not know what he had revealed that night in his intoxication, but having got this far, he decided life could only get better by sharing his problems with her.

"How about giving me some dessert first?"

She smiled, put a wet arm around him and gave him a light hug. "Caramel custard coming right up sir!"

She handed out a large portion in the kitchen, held his hand and led him to the living room. "Here, let me put you on the couch, literally. You will find it more comfortable. I will pull up a chair and sit a safe distance from you. Relax, the custard is not spiked."

Hailing as he did, from a traditional background, he found her open attitude and informal approach unusual. He had grown up in an environment and time that stressed that the only woman you were supposed to touch was your wife, and if you did touch another, it was because you had no morals. He did not mind discussing problems with Neelam freely, but this touch and hug business (while it felt good) made him uncomfortable.

He finished the custard first and wondered where to start. Nirupama, naturally rankled as the most recent problem. He told Neelam about the second encounter with Nirupama and then the first. About his mother and father, his father's premature death, his mother's lonely end in India.

A wide-open, garden-like restaurant in far away Madras, a girl who had ventured there one evening, and the rest of his life story. He casually mentioned that he was a fan of a Bengali actress, as though to explain the presence of photographs, but nothing more. As she listened, he noted her manner had transformed from playful to intense concentration. She rarely interrupted, except to recheck a name or place, and asked him questions in a manner that helped reveal his inner fears.

"Here, have a glass of water," she offered when he completed his chronicle.

"First, thank you for sharing your world with me. I am trying to understand the issues of your life... While I am thinking about what you said, and before I respond, why don't you fill in a few details about your work. The first time you were here, you mentioned you worked for an organization funded by Non-Resident Indians, you said it's non-profit, more like a Trust. I want to know because, where a person works, what he does for a living, is often a reflection of his personality, his covert and overt beliefs. Tell me, what do you do, from 8 to 5."

He told her about his humble role in a noble organisation, Neel Akash, set up to help women live free under the blue sky. Its fight against the social ills of dowry, domestic abuse and rape. Its role in deliverance of women - from stigma, superstition and discrimination. Promoting widow remarriage, which faces opposition even today in some parts of India. Eliminating female infanticide, which still exists.

He told her about the back end, in the US, based at Boulder, Colorado, which he was part of, the nerve centre for data management. How he got the offer when he was in his third year, through an NRI uncle who was a trustee. How the Trust collects funds by asking for just five dollars a month from thousands of NRIs. Collects data on victims through a network of NGOs, socially-inclined lawyers, true feminists and human rights activists who report to the India office in New Delhi any instance of wrong doing against women. Verifies the report through an independent investigation, after which a case number is allocated. Hires lawyers to help destitute or widowed women receive their fair share of property, file divorce proceedings in case of repeated domestic abuse, and criminal suits in cases of rape or dowry.

He could see she was intrigued by his account. And the goals the Trust had set appealed to the woman in her. "How come I have never heard of Neel Akash till now. No one has approached me for a contribution. Why just five dollars a month? People like me will give more..."

"Well, five dollars because you never feel the pinch and you will not refuse, but the money comes from numbers. You may not have been contacted because your name is not yet in our database, and that's my job, building the database and maintaining it online, which can be accessed by our offices across the US.

"We do not have a public face, but we work behind the scenes. In India, you may find us, say in the form of a well-meaning lawyer who will not charge fees, while in reality he would be paid from our corpus. We prefer a low profile because once you become too visible, you either get false claims or allegations."

She was silent for a few minutes. He could see her ruminating, assembling the events of his past, grappling for a sense of his work place, and wondering if she had taken on something bigger than just preparing his evening meal. He knew she was just a housewife trying to play agony aunt, and now she had found that his life was beyond her analysis and advice.

"Let's see what we have," she began confidently. "Your first major setback was the traumatic bereavement, when your father died, because it was not a natural death but murder. From thereon, your system became hyper vigilant, that is almost waiting for the next disaster, and in your life it happened one after another.

"You constantly review in your mind the tragedies of the past. You keep looking for blame. For Nirupama's rejection, you blame womankind; for your father's murder, you blame society; the legal system for not punishing the offender.

"You have done the right thing, with me today. Because, by expressing your grief and grievances, you actually bring light to the dark side of life. Believe me, you can emerge from it wiser and stronger."

He was taken aback. "Wait, you are not just a housewife are you?"

"Just a housewife?" she looked at him quizzically, one mobile eyebrow raised in question, while her eyes danced with mischief. "Did you say you worked for an organization that that wants to eradicate the taboo and oppression against women?" She was teasing him again. He was thoroughly embarrassed.

"Look, I did not mean to be condescending. Housewives are some of the most noble, self-sacrificing...." She interrupted his incoherent defense with a chuckle. "Allow me to finish, young man. It would be nice if you don't interrupt when the analysis is in progress.

"You kept your trauma in a separate compartment so that it could continue to haunt you through your life. Your traumatic experiences were never integrated, processed through normal memory channels. You kept preserving trauma in brine, in its original raw state. With every new trauma, and aided by loneliness, you got re-traumatized. You could have easily handled your cousin last night at Colby. But you kept your past trauma "waiting at the door," re-activated the old memory, allowed the experience to repeat itself. Your mind continues to exert negative influence on your external behavior, whether you like it or not."

Slowly it dawned on him, that she was trained. Either she had led support groups in the community, or she had been through trauma sometime in her life, the treatment of which had transformed her into a capable counselor.

It was now his turn to smile. He folded his hands, settled deeper into the couch and said, "Go on, Dr. Neelam. You may complete your diagnosis."

"Ahem, let's see where we were...You are a classic case of NATs. Negative Automatic Thoughts. Think of everything that has depressed you. You will find that at times your mistake was to make bad things big, big enough to think they have changed your life. When your cousin asked you to leave the first time, it was just part of growing up, getting to know how the other sex reacts in a situation... You made it the turning point of your life!

"Now look at things from a different angle. You kept using binoculars the wrong way, making good things small. You overlook the fact that at an early age you got a chance to take up an assignment in the United States that will change lives in India. Today, from what you said, you are respected at the workplace, yet you write off your success, and focus on your failures.

"You just love to dismiss the good things in your life, take even our relationship... It took me many months to have a word with you, someone living across the door. You don't want any happy experiences.

"You have this habit of jumping to conclusions via mind reading. I spike your drink. Does that mean I want a physical relationship? You people from India, including that cousin of yours, Nirupama, cannot think of anything else, because of your black and white approach to life. There are over a 100 ways to tell someone "I love you," or "I like being with you," without getting physical. And love or liking does not mean just what you think, samjhe, you understand?

"You must learn not to over-generalize and to predict a negative future. One girl rejects you. Does that mean all girls will? I bet, if on the next day, you had gone back to that house in Manda, Mandavel or however you pronounce it, she would have welcomed you, introduced you to her parents. Your life could have turned positive from that point.

"Tell me, now, why did you not go back to her house, because you were afraid she will not receive you?"

"Uh, huh, what did you say?" he sputtered. "Why did I not go back to the girl's house next day or the next week?

"I was afraid she'd think I was taking advantage of her, or she may not have wanted to be reminded of the incident - who knows what women think? I could not have borne it, if she, she too... had thought poorly of me."

"Arjun, you get an A for gallantry, but D for courtship!" Neelam retorted. "For all you know, she wished for you to come back, but coming from that culture, she could never have voiced it. With some women you have to be perceptual, you have to discount the silence, look for non-verbal signs.

"Let's move to a broader level now from that specific instance. Next time you meet a girl who seems to like you, and you like her, try these things. They are simple, day-to-day acts, but will go a long way in sending out a deep non-verbal message.

"Hold her hands, may be give her a hug, but don't crave for the next step. Make sure the other person feels important and respected. Spend time together. Go out for a meal, or do something unexpected or unusual, that makes the relationship more interesting.

"Find out what's special for the other person - and do it! Remember

I made sweet pongal for you? Talk to each other. Listen to fears and concerns, like I am doing now.

"Don't be scared to flirt a little bit. I know I did, but that's the best way of getting to know a man better. Some of the things I tell you may seem alien, because I come from a different background, but remember we are both Indians at heart, and our core values are the same."

He had a new sense of admiration for Neelam. She was different from other women, with whom he had been in contact. Compared to the high strung, paranoid Nirupama, and that docile, vulnerable girl, Neelam was light years ahead in maturity. She would not mistake his presence unlike Nirupama. She would be able to handle a man if he made a pass at her, unlike that poor chiffon girl.

As the opinions crystallized in his mind, he suddenly experienced a sense of shame. Was Nirupama wrong in over-reacting, was the girl at Woodys incapable of taking care of herself? Were they to blame, or was it the environment they grew up in, the traditions that preached an over-blown version of morality and often painted a Dracula picture of men?

Neelam's analysis, so close to the truth, helped him find a new perspective. Life had carried him from the womb to a foreign soil, and along the way he had been bruised, by the death of his father, the stigmas borne by his widowed mother, and the rejection by his cousin. What the world saw was an introvert, a recluse and an outcast. Here was someone who viewed him differently.

"Oh," Neelam exclaimed, interrupting his thoughts. "It's time for my next patient. That will be 100 dollars, please." She held out her hand as though for money, caught his and drew him out of the couch into her arms, holding him for what seemed like ages, comforting him like his mother.

Presently he pulled away, not because he disliked her touch, but because it was starting to feel good being close to her "I will always remember this, Neelam," he said, reading in her eyes care and compassion, something he had been deprived of in his adulthood. "I never expected so much understanding from you."

"Don't make me blush. You know what I am going to do... I am going to give you a treat for sharing your life with me. Treat does not mean just a lunch or dinner at a fancy restaurant. My treat takes the form of "practice what you preach." Remember what I said about doing something unusual... we are going for a picnic, tomorrow."

"Picnic, in this freezing cold?"

"Yes. We are going to a frozen lake on the north side of town. For a picnic on ice."

* * *

Sub Zero, the ice cream parlour on Park Street, Calcutta, is one of the few downtown establishments to have withstood the test of time. In that sense, it compares with Flurys, the delectable confectionery outlet, and Maple, the friendly restaurant, each symbolizing the fascination of Park Street to up-market Calcuttans. Rekha Sen came in to Sub Zero once a week on a Saturday, at about 4 p.m. Normally she would stick to an ice cream soda, while her nephew in tow would plough through a banana split, but today she was indulgent, because she was upset. What the heck, why bother about calories, why look good and for whom... she ordered a double sundae with an extra topping of nuts and chocolate sauce.

She read the print out of his email again. His nervous, staccato response, hid more than what he wrote. That he was never enamoured with Rekha Sen as a person, his admiration was not for her, but for her postponement of aging. She was but a mirror for another woman, whom he pictured as young, and who wanted to stay that way.

He had failed the test: a subtle degeneration in her looks, brought about by trained hands - age lines on her face, sagging chin, grey hair – he had been upset to see his icon destroyed. And what if his fantasy woman too were to reflect Rekha Sen's withered looks... his mail expressing concern at her sudden aging, revealed his inner anguish for the safety of his preserved image.

In reality, she should have been angry with Arjun. He had treated her as just another mashe peshe whom he could use when convenient. As a true blue Bengali from a matriarchal society, it was her wont to dominate, and take no nonsense from men. This atypical trait she knew

101

worked the other way too, with men expecting their mothers to fawn over them, and in turn the dominating wives forever plotting to take the upper hand.

Back to Arjun. She could not get angry with a man who was so childlike. She wished she could enter his troubled mind, discover the tempest that had blown in his youth, the calamity that must have befallen in his childhood. Unearth the hopes he cherished for the future, and nurtured in contemporary images. And understand why he would never allow his dream girl to grow old.

She knew him by now, he would have quickly replaced her with another well-preserved icon. Losing Arjun was not a case of one admirer less, for in the two years, she had hung on to him too... hoping that as she made a comeback, there would be hundreds like him, writing to her regularly, always awaiting her reciprocation. He had been the herald of her future fan following.

Such is life, Rekha Sen pondered wryly, a series of subliminal compromises, for our own intimate ends. And on the lighter side, she pondered again, this time with a smile, as to whom he would have found: a well-fed southie actress with thunder thighs. Sure he would be back, because they get fat fast.

Thinking of Arjun, you could not dwell long on the lighter side. His long, brooding letters came to her mind, his recounting of his childhood days in Madras, his description of his father and mother, his rambling about the streets he loved, the places he frequented. She had a mental picture of his native city: quiet, laid back, conservative, crawling with vegetarians, a city where fish was more likely found in the aquarium than at the dining table. She knew the school where he studied, his college, the ground and gymnasium where he worked out and the eateries he frequented. That garden type restaurant he often wrote about, she wondered why he was so fixated with it. He never wrote about women, although she once playfully brought up the subject, asking why he wrote more of places than people. He had ignored her query.

With the test bringing home the truth, with communication at a standstill, and faced with the self-demeaning option of reminding him to reply, Rekha Sen decided the situation called for a drastic change of strategy, an act that would prove her good intent, and bring Arjun back to the fold.

A solution that might defy logic, not stand to reason, but emanate from the heart. To arrive at its zenith, she would awaken her inner spirit, open the trapdoors deep within and retrieve the answer that lay innermost. She knew the perfect environment to nurture this thought process. A place she had been to, incognito, during her heyday, seeking solace when faced with the dilemma of accepting a producer's offer, of becoming his unlawfully wedded second wife. She had starred in four films under the banner of his company, they had been to foreign locales together, she had spent quality time at his Tollygunge guest house, and over time she had decided he would make a good husband, albeit second hand. She was contemplating saying yes, when he arrived at her apartment one night. Slurred speech and unsteady gait. Behaviour typical of a married man in the midst of an affair, she said to herself as she led him to the couch – propose marriage, regret, and drink to forget. Were there at least some men who were not stereotypes? Presently, she pleaded a sudden attack of migraine and asked him to leave, summoning the driver to ensure he rode down the lift without passing out.

The next morning, devoid of make up and expensive attire, she had driven in her brother's car to Ramakrishna Temple at Belurmath, Howrah, on the banks of the Ganga. The temple houses the relics of Sri Ramakrishna Paramahamsa, and was envisioned by Swami Vivekananda as a tribute to the Great Master. She entered the Naatmandira, or congregational hall, picked a far corner, and sat cross legged, taking the first step towards divine assistance.

She was religious, not spiritual. She had no guru, she had not been initiated, but she knew the cardinal principles of meditation: Switch off thoughts, shut out the world, ascend, ascend, higher and higher, till the soul reaches the apex of the universe. For over 15 minutes she had focused on draining her heart and soul, creating a vacuum that contained no questions or answers, people or places, problems or solutions. In that supreme state, the answer emerged as one word: Crockery.

Why get into a situation that will lead to flying saucers in two homes? Why believe something will work when even the start is not right? Why hurt another woman to please herself? And why, why trust a man, who says he will marry first and divorce later? Here was a sordid combination of debauchery and treachery, packaged as a harried husband seeking a second chance.

Seated cross legged on the same spot, some six years later, her sixth sense heightened by prayer and meditation, she perceived the first rays of a warm light. It enveloped the universe she was perched in, surrounding a gray sphere with a yellow glow. From nowhere came the words: The answer to Arjun is Arjun himself. Go back, relive his past. Absorb the places familiar and comforting to him. Enter his lost world, that part of the past he treasures most, and partake the sights and sounds of his favourite city. Share your perceptions of his past, which would help communicate the empathy that he craves from women.

Comforted by the revelation, she began the slow descent from the pinnacle to the Earth, gently landing on the mat. The logic seemed more apparent as she reached home. In a converse way, what was important to him should matter to her. Does not a good wife wish to percolate into her husband's environment?

Was that her subconscious motive, she wondered... a fast forward of action, humoring her current thinking? Would she get to wear the red and white bangles she coveted every time she passed the shops at Kalighat? Would she be able to hold Arjun's arm and walk down Roland Road, take him to Bengal Club for lunch on Sundays or take it easy at the lake side as Arjun da jogged around Rabindra Sarobar? The possibility of marriage in the near future and proud jaunts to her home town possessed her as she planned the first step in her Madras trip, nestling in a sheer white satin night robe amid lilac coloured cushions on her living room divan.

She knew he was in love with another woman, and she knew he liked her because she was the alter ego. The thought did not irk her, for a practical reason. The woman he had in mind would be married, and Arjun da's sense of morality would only keep him pining, he would never make advances, he would never meet her discreetly and come home with perfect alibis. What about the fact that until now he had used her? Well, was that something unusual to the gender? Arjun had been a shade kinder, he had used her from afar, without the hallmarks of the leverage men are infamous for: false promises, intimate contact, and a temporary place as Biwi No. 1 or 2.

What about other ground realities, the difference in their backgrounds and culture? They were poles apart, he wouldn't meet her halfway, she would have to cross over. Arjun, virgin, she far from it. Tall, muscular, melancholy. Above average height, voluptuous, outspoken. Fond of Bengali sweets. Fond of all things sweet. Liked being with attractive, well-preserved women. Liked being with strong, silent men. Searching for the right man, to marry and settle down. Searching for the right woman, already married and settled down.

If at all there was a flipside, it was a frivolous yet formidable one.

Food. Fish if you wish. Well, giving it up should be no big deal. Maybe she could keep some tinned salmon at home, and cook it when he travelled. Or she could eat out once a week, alone. Or she could explain that among Bengalis, even Brahmins ate fish, and by derivation it should not be considered non-vegetarian. Or she could develop a set of Bengali friends wherever she had to live, and find a way to visit them by turn once or twice a week. Forget it, she could not live without mache jol, just as he wouldn't without curd rice. Separate kitchens should do the trick.

Back to the trip. The only city Rekha Sen had been to in the South was Bangalore, en route to a shoot at the verdant Brindavan Gardens, Mysore. She had just one contact in Madras, a veteran director who had served with her on the panel of a jury for the National Film Awards. She found he was away abroad on a film shoot, but his helpful son-in-law came on the line, and offered his hospitality, including a car and a Hindi-speaking driver during her stay. She looked forward to the sojourn for other reasons too… she had the time, money and now the inclination. She was very much bored with life, tired of waiting for that dream call from directors.

She landed two days later, checked into Woodlands, next to a hotel called Savera. For the first few days, she let herself go, doing nothing in particular, sleeping and waking late, enjoying the Udupi style vegetarian food, going for long walks in the evening, from the hotel to the beach and back. One night, to satiate the carnivore in her, she opted for a change of cuisine. She entered Hotel Chola, which she had spotted during her meandering, asked for the Coffee Shop, which strangely enough was located on the first floor. She entered The Mercara, ordered and gratefully put away a plate of crisp fried fish with creamy tartar sauce.

As she reached the lobby from the coffee shop, she was sure she saw an apparition. Someone resembling Arjun, rather a person with a similar build, shoulders to be precise, exiting through the swing doors. Her spirit soared on seeing the broad blades, because that was the best part of Arjun's anatomy she had noticed first when she met him the first time. She wanted to have a closer look, but a taxi picked up the person and moved away. In the front seat, there had been a young boy and a woman, probably a maid. Her mind was too full of Arjun. She had to be careful not to mistake every tall broad shouldered man for him. Somewhat dejected, she returned to her hotel, making a mental note to return next day and ask if by any chance a Mr. Arjun was staying at the hotel. It was nicer to postpone the query than to ask now and be disappointed.

The following morning, after soaking in the spirit of the city, she decided to proceed on the trail, the trail of young Arjun.

His school was on a road named Habibullah Road, at a place called T. Nagar (what did T stand for?) He had the habit of describing places so well in his letters, she felt she had been there before. He would state the road name, landmarks, adjoining roads and such. She suspected that the detailed description of his familiar locations gave him a sense of control, which children find when a story is repeated every night with the same minute details. In the process, over the two years, she could pinpoint Woodys, his school, college, family home, and the police headquarters where his father had served. She tried to recall the mail about his school:

Venkatasubbarao High School. A boy's school near a famous girls school called Vidhyodaya. Most boys from T. Nagar went either to my school or PSBB in the adjoining Lake Area. It's been 23 years, I wonder how much has changed... Mani the head peon must have retired, the head master is no more I heard. Sorry to load you with trivia... let me tell you about Pondy Bazar in T.Nagar, you must go there if you ever visit Madras. It's a bustling market place, full of shops. Don't miss Geeta Bhavan, mornings around seven am, you will find the production assistants of film crews, taking away breakfast in jumbo size tiffin carriers. There is a theatre too... named Rajkumari, you know it is named after an actress of yesteryears who owns it (you should put up one in Calcutta). The bus stop is called "Power House," possibly because a sub station is located nearby. I hear another actor has put up a theatre near the first one. It is called Nagesh. Opposite the theatre is a convent school called Holy Angels...

Aided by his communication and her silver screen background, and now being on location, she could visualize the scenes of his past easily:

Arjun alighting from the bus at Habibullah Road (Route 13-A), dressed in Binny white and khaki shorts, strolling with school bag slung like a backpack. Now among 20-odd boys in the playground, playing baseball, or "round cricket" as Arjun would describe it, Why the name 'round cricket?' Because you hit the baseball, and as opposed to American baseball where the striker would run, in the Indian version, he stayed put, counting runs by circling the bat swiftly around his waist, one round of the bat, one run. There goes the final bell, over a hundred students exit in a mad rush, as though there is no school tomorrow. Here comes Arjun, he nears the vendor selling Magnolia ice cream, buys a choco-bar, and walks home relishing the slow melt of the chocolate layer in his mouth.

She smiled, as she stood unobtrusively near the school gate for she knew he had been happy when his mother and father were alive, with no women messing up his life. Those women, or woman, who had entered his life at some point of time, were probably still around, right here in Madras, may be a few kilometres from where she stood, blissfully unaware of the trauma they had caused or the hope they had kindled in his mind.

She sighed, praying to Durga Ma to set right his future. She made a pledge - to feed 500 orphans if he ever found resolution.

Next was his college, a Jesuit institution off Sterling Road, from the look of it, one of the finest in the city, catering to a cosmopolitan student profile. She could see him keeping away from the guitar-strumming groups, the pot-smoking crowd, and the cliques that happily whiled away time over tea and cigarettes at Kuttys. She could picture him attentive in class, on the first row (alphabetical seating), and active in athletics and volleyball, but not in annual culturals like "Down Sterling."

The in thing among boys in my class was "dating, she recalled him writing: *There were various levels and versions those days: group dates, four boys, four girls going out for an evening, kicking off with a film at Devi Paradise, followed by dinner at Buharis. The bolder ones would not need the shelter of a group, they would go out with a girl to Nine Gems ice cream parlor on Edward Elliots Road, and then to the Marina Beach for a stroll and if the stretch was desolate enough, hold hands and get cozy. The radicals would go one step further: Take the girl out to Silversands on a Saturday morning, rent a cottage for the day. I can't imagine what the boy and girl would say to the parents on returning home... that they have been busy with combined studies?*

Last his family home, tucked deep in T. Nagar (ah, T stood for Theagaraya), on the perimeter of a playground named Somasundaram ground. She knew that the home was kept locked, and that Arjun did not want to sell or rent it. His mother's brother would come in once a month with a servant, dust the house, and ensure it stayed rodent-free.

She knew a second key was with the neighbour, fortunately a Mr. Ganguly. Three minutes of fast talk in Bengali, laced with the latest personal details about Arjun, convinced Ganguly da that she was a family friend from Calcutta who might move in to take care of the house. He opened the door for her, invited her for a cup of tea after she was through, and left. The uncle must be a fastidious man, she said to herself as she moved around. It was spick and span, from corner to corner. Her heart reached out to Arjun when she saw the framed photos on the wall. *His father in police uniform. Young Arjun on a holiday with his parents. His father receiving a medal of honour.* Moments of pride, happiness and family history, captured on film by Agfa.

What were the words he used to describe his house? A treasurehouse of memories. He had spent happy days within this two-ground plot. Crawled up the stairs, holding on to the banister, late at night, to seek the comfort of his mother's arms. He had the traditional and symbolic oil bath early morning on Diwali day and donned new clothes before setting out to the garden to burst the mightiest and loudest crackers his father could buy. Celebrated Pongal, the harvest festival, on January 14. She could almost capture the aroma, taste the jaggery-laden, nut garnished sweet dish as she surveyed the barren kitchen two decades later.

When she returned to Gangulyda's house to give him back the keys, she found the entire family waiting for her, his aged mother, his wife and two children, who had appeared from nowhere in ten minutes.

"Didi, didi," Ganguly da was almost in tears. "I am sorry. I never expected that you of all people would land up in Madras, that too at my house. I kept wondering why you look so familiar. Can we please take a photograph with you? And you must stay and have a meal with us. Today we have fish, luckily your favourite dish, mache jol."

* * *

CHAPTER SIX

The hero can go forth of his own volition to accomplish the adventure...

or he may be carried or sent abroad by some benign or malignant

agent.

Icicles on trees. Snow chains on tires. Breath misting into vapor. Colorado in the grip of winter.

They exited the cold, clean roads of Boulder and merged into the northbound Interstate. Neelam was driving a Pajero, and he could appreciate the value of a high power, all terrain 4-wheel drive on a day like this. For the snow was reaching earthward in a torrent of flakes. "We are heading into a snow storm," he said weakly, not sure if she would pay heed, for by now it was clear that at that point in his life, she was totally in control.

"Arjun, don't be a wimp. If you get wet in the rain, you don't melt... we are not made of sugar. And nothing happens if you are out in the snow either, as long as you don't do a strip tease." She reached out and squeezed the muscles on his arm, through the cardigan. "When the going gets tough, the tough get going, terrible cliché, but great timing right?"

He wanted to add: "get going home," but decided against it. Then she would pull over and give him a reassuring hug – tempting but avoidable.

As they neared the lake, as though on cue, the flakes petered out, presenting a clear view of the cold, clean lake surface. They parked on the deserted fringe, alongside a fir tree. Neelam left the engine running, to keep the cabin warm. From the rear, she pulled out a thermo-heated hamper, and they embarked, for what she had promised, a true picnic on ice.

"Hang on, before we enter the lake, first thing we do is test the surface." She held his hand and they gingerly we stepped in, to make sure it was frozen and not just covered with a thin sheet of ice, a probability in winter.

"Yipee, it's really hard on top." She placed the hamper on the surface and did a short war dance with more cries of "Yipee, Yipee, ya, ya." He could only conclude that married women are at their bubbly best when the husband is not around.

"This going to be a short picnic by the way, sort of a microcosm of a real one. He was stumped as before by her vocabulary, and antonym of the typical housewife image. "Don't look at me like that, microcosm is the opposite of macrocosm and means that we are looking at a larger image in its microscopic size. Sure you know the meaning, but this is just to say I know too, ha ha!

"Ok, getting back from English lecture to our picnic plans, we are going to spend quality time out here. Because beyond five minutes, we are going to be history. Let me pour a cup of steaming coffee for you, and you can munch a Snickers along with it."

As he drew warmth from her open manner and the hot beverage, he marvelled at her adventurous spirit. Why can't more women be like her - no inhibitions, hang-ups or ulterior motives, only true friendship.

"What are you thinking Arjun?"

"Appreciating you, and the picnic idea," he retorted frankly. She liked that, for she beamed with pleasure. She collected his empty cup and candy wrapper, and stowed them carefully in the hamper along with hers. To his surprise, she pulled out a box of matches.

"Relax, I am not going to smoke, nor will I ask you to. We will try an exercise, and we have maybe three minutes before we freeze. I will ask you a question. The moment I finish, you will strike a match, hold it up between your fingers. Answer the question before the flame burns out. That is, you have time till the flame reaches your finger, and after that naturally you will tend to drop the match. As you have very little time, you will be forced to skip the chaff and get to the grain. Get the gloves off and let's start, buster."

Her sudden announcement caught him by surprise. But it was too late, and too cold to argue. He stuffed his gloves into the overcoat pockets, pulled the parka type hood tighter over his head, and held the match in ready-to-strike position.

"Question one: What do you like most about women?"

Match flares, flame holds steady in the still air. Frozen lake, lone tree, Neelam, the Mitsubishi and him. Clean air, clear mind.

"Their vulnerability. Because I see them as a gender weaker than men. Physically, surely, and mentally, behind all their façade, they are not as strong.

"I want to be their protector. That is why I get hurt when they see me as the enemy. "

Flame reaches flesh. Now Neelam's turn to strike, his to ask.

"What do you like most in men?"

"The fact they are dumb when it comes to women. They don't understand women very well, but make a noise that they do. That makes them lovable because they can be so silly. I enjoy correcting them, like I am doing with you.

"Your turn, and here is the question.

"What part of a woman, and I mean physical, turns you on most?"

He gulped. "Na, na, Arjun, you are not allowed to think, we want top of the mind answer, and you give me the world's best known response, I will brand you a lecher, samjhe?" she added playfully, as he hastened to strike the match.

"No, it's not what you think. What I like are the eyes. The more intense, the better. Some women have eyes that twinkle, some are deadpan. I look for intensity, for the warmth that radiates from the inner soul."

"Your turn, doctor." His turn to be playful.

"Ok, my answer to the physical part I like in men… here goes the match.

"It's not what you think either. I go for the nose, because it says all you need to know about a man. Firm, big but not bulbous, closer to aquiline, that's the mark of mental strength. If it's set in a clear face without a moustache, I can admire the man for hours.

"Last one minute, before we freeze, get set with your match. Tell me Arjun, what is the single most ambition, that drives you on and on?"

He did not have to wait for the match to burn through to finish. His life goal spilled out in a single line:

"I want to marry her. Too late, I know, but that's' what I want most in life."

Looking back to that cold winter afternoon, despite many mental reviews and replays, he was never sure who among the two had started what happened next. He knew he had lowered his voice to a whisper and stepped closer to her, as though he feared being overheard. He knew he had said every word with clear diction because he could not have repeated the sacrilegious statement.

He could see the vapors of their breath mingling before dissipating, he was glad her well executed strategy had led to exchange of their inner selves. She had succeeded in letting out the deepest thought in his heart. The genesis must have been that singular moment of expression, when his brain, or hers, conveyed the signal to the nervous system, to bond physically with one who had bonded cerebrally, causing arms to rise in unison, and hold each other tight, tighter, tightest.

He realized at that moment that the touch is an extension of mental communion, and an emotional act, not a carnal one. The attestation of a universal truth: a true relationship transcends the physical, forging a bond of love, true love for a fellow human being.

He wanted the moment to last, frozen in time like the sheet of ice on the lake surface. Last forever, to protect him from his tormentors, like the lake surface holding them firm and safe from the icy water deep below.

If only the world would stand still, like the motionless fir at the lake fringe, if only he could turn his guiding light into a destination....

Her finger on his blood. First contact with body fluid. Lingering of her finger a fraction longer. Embryonic act demanding its natural end. His perpetual endeavor to complete the cycle.

Neelam is saying something. He does not hear even in the pin drop

113

silence that rings through the still atmosphere. Her gloved palms are digging into his shoulders, and she is holding him closer. Her lips are moving, and they seem to repeat the same words:

"Kiss me, Arjun. Just once, and we will forget about it forever. If you don't, I will, even if it is an insult to my femininity."

He attempts to draw away, but her hands are now holding his shoulders firm. He struggles, and suddenly, she lets go, all her desire deflated by his reluctance.

"I should have known it, you will forever suffer with that image within. Let me tell you the truth, that girl is no angel for you, but your mother's alter ego. You vicariously seek from her what you received from your mother.

"You are bound by the walls of childhood. You still want to be dandled upon your mother's knees. Unless you overcome your fixations and the emotional impotence caused by infantile affect, you will forever remain a child."

Neelam removing mittens, rubbing her hands together, placing her warm palms on his cheek. "They don't make people like you any more. You belong to a Shakespearean world. You have the madness of Macbeth, the obsession of Hamlet, the passion of Antony. The final truth is Oedipus rules your behaviour, and that's not a character in Shakespeare, I am afraid.

"Don't ask me to explain how I know so much about you. That's not relevant now, what you need to do is to resolve your inner conflicts, and fast. Return to your past…. Find the answers to your burning questions. In the process, you may discover yourself. Like water in this frozen lake, the true self lies deep, deep below in our heart. Promise me, that you will go back. Go on the trail, the trail of young Arjun. Meet people whom you adore, visit places you love most.

"Let me know, big man… I am curious to hear… how your mystical journey turns out."

* * *

CHAPTER SEVEN

Plants come to blossom, but only to return to the root.

Neelam had been right. To resurrect, to change, to emerge anew, I had to return to my roots. I had to complete the truncated journey - to discover my true identity. Unleash the hidden memories, exorcise the bitter experiences trapped within, to find freedom from an old captivity.

I had to retrace the warm and hurting moments by physical presence... in the corridors of my past. There were doors either side, some white, some black, a few gray. Some had golden handles that gently descended upon my touch, some had twisted steel that refused to budge.

I had summoned the mental strength to open a few, yet there were others I had refrained from, like my parental home on the perimeter of Somasundaram ground, locked since my mother's death, not to be sold, not to be rented, but retained until such time I could come to terms with its empty confines, and find a way to fill it with happiness.

Spurred by the visit to my mother's school, nostalgic with the recapture of her early days, and drawing solace from the warm touch of the ground that once held her feet, I took the next bold step: I visited the abode where my mother had lived for many years under the shelter of my grand uncle.

I knew from family sources that he was alive, and probably my mother's only living blood relative. I remembered him from my youth. I remembered him as an appalam unit owner, caterer and my mother's redeemer. Sathyamangalam Sambasiva Iyer.

I wondered how difficult it would have been for my grandmother when Sambasiva Iyer offered to support my mother. On one side the monetary issue, making sense for a widowed, almost destitute woman to accept that her daughter could live with her brother. On the other, the trauma of giving away an offspring whom you very much want to retain and raise, because the little one was the only valuable possession you had.

With two mouths to feed, and money hardly for one, the choice is not difficult. Logic overcomes emotion. Still, I knew she showered her love in ways that she could. She would take her daughter home on Sundays, give her an oil bath, feed her hot pepper rasam, fried appalam and potato roast, and try to make up in one day all that she had missed for the week. Tears would well in the mother's eyes as the evening shadows fell; she would recover and bid farewell. Next Sunday was only six days away.

Strangely, I had never been to my uncle's house. I think my father for certain reasons had not been too willing to take me there, wanting to keep the distance between me and my mother's early days. Unlike me, he believed in burying the past.

As I stepped in for the first time in my 40 years, I felt I had been there before. It was a typical West Mambalam home, except it was larger than the rest. The past of my past had spent time here, anguished, hoped and prayed within this very brick and mortar. As I entered the hall, I realized why a large house had been necessary in the first place. The hall housed an appalam making unit, meaning all the people who make the appalams for my uncle worked herein. There must have been 12 women, young, middle age and two grandmotherly women, obviously the veterans among the lot, who were busy rolling out appalams from balls of dough. The rolling pins in their hands moved with practiced perfection, creating almost perfect circles of appalams, which were then placed on spreadsheets of newspaper, to be taken later to the terrace for drying. I stood transfixed at the sight, not because it was stunning prima facie, but because of its import.

My mother would have rolled out the dough like these women. Sure, it was a respectable occupation for the lower strata of my community, it gave them two meals a day, and money to buy at least rice and meager provisions, it was better than moaning over one's plight at home, yet what struck me in the scene was its continuum. In this new millennium that boasts of computer literacy and cutting edge technology, something had to be done to change the lives of such women, someone had to find them a new way to earn a living. Some day, if I had my way, I would change their lives to run in tandem with the New World.

Visitors are unusual I suppose at appalam making units, except for storeowners or their representatives stepping in to place orders. Especially well built visitors, over six feet, with short hair and the looks of a policeman. One by one the nine pins stopped rolling as eyes turned, and one maker whispered to another.

"I came to see Sambasiva Iyer," I announced to no one in particular. "I am his relative, I have come from America."

No response. Thoughtfully, I added, "My mother used to work here many years ago. Her name is Marakatham."

The name meant nothing to the younger ones. But the oldest of the lot slowly rose and came towards me. She looked me over from face to toe and then returned her nostalgic gaze to my face. "You are Marakatham's son," she said as though affirming my antecedents. "You have her eyes, the same mouth, and the lost look she always had."

"Patti, is my uncle here?"

"He has gone out, kolande. His daughter is up in the terrace, just go up these stairs. Hmmm, after so many years I feel as though I am seeing Marakatham again in your roop, how I wish she was alive…"

I climbed up the stairs, pulled open a half closed door and stepped right into another page of history. Appalam, vattal, and salted lime drying in the hot sun. Uncle's daughter on the terrace, crouched under an umbrella, Deepavali Malar magazine in hand.

As I set foot on the terrace, I was transported back in time to a scene I had never witnessed yet lay stored within, Time granted me the supreme boon of reversal, while spirits from the past reunited with their progeny, eliciting a strange sense of elation. Of all the significant moments in my mystical trail – setting foot on my mother's school, seeing the eyes of Arumugham, revisiting the girl's home - this was the most magical, because the reward was greater than finding the Holy Grail.

"Neenga yaru?" the voice of my cousin, breaking the spell. Eerie but true, I had heard this before.

"I am your cousin, I live in America, I am Marakatham's son."

"Oh, vaango, appa is not at home," she said in a mixture of Tamil and English, typical of Madras. "Please come down to the hall. Have a cup of coffee."

* * *

She looked at me curiously as I approached the porch. They say that after 30, a man gains around two pounds every year, and will keep gaining unless he stays active and in shape. I had put on at least 7 kilos in the last 20 years, most of it muscle. My hair was shorter, and I had shaved off the moustache I sported during college days.

I knew she would never recognize or expect after all these years. In her mind, at that moment, I was one of many who struggle to find an address in Anna Nagar. It's a neighbourhood not divided by streets, but by sectors, or by alphabets that represent sectors. Which means if you are looking for U-42, you need to find U first and then simply look around in the hope of finding house No. 42. A passerby stopping to ask for directions is very common.

To my surprise, she spoke first, asking a question:

"Umm, forgive me … are you from my husband's factory? The union staff came last week."

"Er, no, no. I came to meet you. You see, we've met before. I mean, you know me," I fumbled for the one liner and found it: "We met one day, 20 years ago, at Woodys, I dropped you home." I dug into my pocket and pulled out her handkerchief that I had picked up from the floorboard of the auto 20 years ago - embroidered with the letter R and wet with her tears.

She leaned against the porch, covered her face with her palms for a moment, drew them down to her neck, and looked at me deeply, adding back the moustache, deducting the extra pounds. "Yes, I remember," she said slowly, measuring out the words, as though to bridge the two decades lost in time. "Why don't you come in?"

I guessed the husband was not at home. I could hear a girl reciting a poem in an adjoining room, and the boy interrupting in between.

My life had been a lonely one. I was glad she had experienced joy. A spacious home, two children, and possibly, since not everyone gets the short end as I do, a caring husband. Thoughts ran deep, speech remained casual, almost superficial.

"I have been living in the United States all this while. I was looking up people I knew. I recalled our meeting. That's why I traced you, just to see how you are. I assure you my intentions are strictly honourable."

"I don't need proof of that. You have already proved you are a gentleman when you helped me, dropped me at home, and never came back, which anyone else would have. You got hurt helping me, and you never used that to your advantage," she responded.

A compliment from someone I cherished so much. Felt good, took me by surprise. I had always seen her only from my perspective; this fresh angle, her evaluation of my attributes, had not crossed my mind. I had assumed that like most women, she was least concerned about forming a positive opinion. "Tell me about yourself," she continued. "How big is your family, has your wife come with you to India?"

I heard the question, but the brain would not relay an answer. I was spellbound by her voice. The pitch, neither low nor high, but a plateau somewhere in between. I relished the audio, and I knew, I would hear the replay at leisure, because every part of her was embedded deep within.

"Well… I, I, I am a bachelor."

It was my turn to ask about her husband, but I overlooked the courtesy. It is one of those things difficult to explain and easy to understand. In my heart she was single. I was not ready to fill in the details of her married life. She did not talk about it either, during the 10 minutes I spent with her.

As we switched between conversation and silence, as we took turns at studying the floor, as the bright lights of the well-furnished home shone on her, I observed her without appearing obvious. More than just being beautiful, she had character. A hidden strength that had been weakened just for a moment, when trapped in an environment out of sync with hers. I was happy to see her here, because this was where she belonged. She was a family person through and through, the kind of daughter fathers dote upon, the little girl who grows up to take charge of a surviving parent, the wife who would stand by her husband through thick and thin, and the mother who raises children who make a difference to their world.

She offered me coffee, but I declined, opting for a glass of water. A hot beverage would have to be made, would take time to consume. I did not want to meet her husband in case he returned from office, factory or wherever.

My mission was accomplished. I was happy for her, but not sure of my state. What had I expected her to say? "Oh, thanks for coming back. I was just planning to divorce my husband, and you just walked in… Or, "I must tell you the truth, I never got married, I actually adopted my sister's children after she died of cancer." My thoughts were too ridiculous to entertain. I wanted to exit, return to my lonely world of hope and despair, and pound tar next morning.

While she was in the kitchen, I could not help looking around the room. There was the usual showcase, typical of Madras, filled with curios, some crockery and two framed photographs in one corner. One must have been of her parents, from the faded look of it, and the contemporary one was her family, taken when the children were infants. Much as I did not want to, I could not stop myself from looking at the spouse's image on her left. I recognised him without much effort.

Sudhakar, from whom I had saved her that evening.

Behind, I could hear the sound of glass being placed on the side table. When I turned around, she knew my question. "He came to my college the next day. He waited for me to come out. Apologised for his behaviour. By that time, I had heard so much about him, that I would not even believe his words. But he pursued me for a month after that. He was rich and spoilt. I wanted to take it as a challenge to reform him, so I started responding to him. We were married a few years later, after I finished my masters."

She stopped abruptly, and broke into tears. I did not have to hear the rest. I knew the standard trap: Good girl meets bad boy, he seems to turn over a new leaf, she gives in to his wants, or in some cases marries him, and later finds out it was all a facade. Games men like to play with women who are difficult to lure.

I drank the water quickly and placed the glass back on the table, finding the appropriate moral to my life story: Nice guys go to hell.

We stood for a moment facing each other. I realized then I would never see her again. All that I could capture of her face before I bid farewell, I would have to retain in my memory for the rest of my life. Her bank manager, her grocer, neighbour, they would meet her, interact with her... daily, or several times a month, and here I was – the man who wanted to see her most, and most often – being sent out of her life in the next few seconds.

I knew she would say, 'Nice meeting you after a long time.' I did not expect her to say, 'Please drop in any time.' She never was good at that. At the risk of appearing impolite, I scanned her closely, and because I wanted to capture her, my eyes moved from head to toe, taking in the still slender build, bright skin, and sunlit face that had resided in my heart for 20 years.

And just for that single moment, my thoughts turned from emotional to physical. Surfacing from deep within, was something unusual - an unjust desire to make her mine. I wished I could step closer, and encircle my arms around her and whisper in her ear the thought that ricocheted in my heart: "You are beautiful."

Given the ground realities, my parting line was mundane. "I am happy I met you again. I need to get back to my motel, I mean hotel. You take care. And take it easy." How much we hold in our heart, how little we express.

"I appreciate your coming here after all these years. Sorry, on that day... I did not ask your name. You are Mr....

"My name is Arjun... If I may ask, what is yours?"

"Ranjini... Rasika Ranjini."

* * *

As Jambu cranked the starter, as I settled deeper into the rear seat, resisting tears and myriad implausible thoughts, I fought the urge to alight, and reenter her home and life. I prayed for the supreme boon to put the clock back, to reverse age, time and events, and to start all over again from the moment I dropped her home, 20 years ago. I longed to be transported to a fairy tale world where ogres turn into helpers, wishes morph into horses, and frogs into princes. Yet, logic warned this was real life, and the princess would forever be out of reach.

What if the Gods could suspend time, freeze the rest of the world except the two of us, and allow me to enter her habitat for just a day? Be with her from morn to night, watch her in gentle motion, tending to her daily chores. To sit with her across the table and share a meal, hear her voice, savour the pitch. Even as I wished, I felt like the frog, which, in all its innocence, had asked the princess a few favors in exchange for retrieving the golden ball from the depths of the pond.

I winced as I recalled what the princess had said to herself on hearing the pleas: "How that simple frog chatters! There he sits in the water with his own kind, and could never be the companion of a human being." A mortal aspiring for an angel would meet a similar fate. All I could do was to ask Jambu to drive away into the cool January night.

* * *

CHAPTER EIGHT

The encounter and separation, for all its wildness, is typical of the sufferings of love... Forces... will have been set in motion beyond the reckoning of the senses. Sequences of events from the corners of the world will generally draw together, and the miracles of coincidence will bring the inevitable to pass.

January is a significant month for many reasons. The month I suffered humiliation at Nirupama's home and met the girl at Woodys. In the same month many years later, my mother left for her heavenly abode, and it is therefore in January her Shraddham ceremony falls due.

I am not much of a believer in rituals, nor am I an atheist, I am probably a non-conformist who accepts the existence of God but questions the conduct of rites and rituals. At times, I wonder if it is a farce, a practice set up to ensure the livelihood of the priestly clan who hold center stage in the ceremonies. For this reason, I rarely wear the sacred thread, though I was initiated into its secrets and symbols at the right age of 11, two years before my father died. So much so, as the first anniversary approached, I was faced with the dilemma of performing her Shraddham, or give it a go by, in line with my views.

I opted for a via media instead. Through Inspector Kumaravel, I paid a one-time amount to a Samaj in Madras, in return for which they would perform the necessary rites on the given day every year for my father and mother. And as most of us know, the day is not necessarily the calendar date of death, but dependent on the birth star of the deceased. Which brings us back to January. My digital diary had reminded me a day earlier that on Jan. 17 falls my mother's ceremony as per the astro calendar. Being right here in Madras, feeling fairly guilty of neglecting a son's duty, and not wanting to anguish the soul further, I decided that this time I would perform the rites personally, rather than by proxy. The culmination of this thought process was my instruction to Jambu to appear at 5 a.m. at the hotel portico. I gave him the address of the Samaj and asked him to inform the priest on his way home.

The hotel informed me that while their service was round the clock, the gymnasium was not. Except Monday, I start all other days with a run, no matter an early flight, no matter late return from work. I would have no option but to run on the road at 3.30 a.m.

Room service woke me up at 3 a.m. with a cup of coffee. Key deposited with the reception 3.25 a.m. Warm up in the portico for four minutes. Kick off towards the beach at precisely 3.30 a.m. The January air is cool. Sodium vapour lights cast a golden glow on tar as I cross the Buckingham Canal bridge and approach the Marina.

Mind at rest, I can't reason why. Maybe I am looking forward to the union with my mother's spirit. Maybe the reunion with my native city has smoothened the rough edges in my heart. Maybe there is a turning point looming in the horizon.

Gandhi Statue ahead. On impulse I run straight past the statue towards the sand. Pace slows, as my shoes form imprints on the sand. I must keep running, towards enlightenment. I reach the breakers, it's firmer here unlike the loose beach sand. I make a perpendicular turn and run northward, parallel to the shoreline. Catamarans and boats silent on the sand. No fishermen, just a bright full moon, and an effervescent sea. A golden moment so close to the truth that I want told.

My shoes, socks, feet are wet - I do not bother to skirt the breakers. Nothing matters now except the bonding with nature, on this lonely waterfront, at this wide-open temple of Nature. I want to get closer to the elements, in body and spirit. Invoke the blessings of the earth, water and the wind, win the empathy of the moon and stars. In deference, I remove my vest, slowing down just a little, and tie it around my waist. The moon beam bounces off my glistening shoulders, the January air nips the warm skin. Bare in the chest, light at heart, almost puritan in form, I pray the Gods above will take notice of this mortal, running with hope at this pre dawn hour.

As though by divine prompting, my mind returns to the reunion with the girl. What did I see, what did I miss? Did I listen, but not hear? Everything was normal… and yet… The waves continue to whisper, but the senses fail to retrieve the truth hidden by the hand of fate.

Vivekananda House on my left. I must return to the road, return to my temporary abode and prepare for the reunion with my mother's spirit. Light the holy fire, chant mantras, and appease the departed soul. 'I am sorry amma, I have denied your due – your soul must have longed all these years for a solemn shradanjali.'

Back at Chola. Key from the front desk. Strip down in the room. Alternate streams of hot and cold water from the shower jet open and close the pores, rejuvenate and refresh and the mind. Clean, clean, clean, inside and out. Wipe dry. Wrap dhoti tight around my waist. Retrieve sacred thread from my suitcase, pass it over the head and right arm, to rest across the left shoulder and body. As I confirm whether I have worn the thread correct or converse, I recall its import: The symbol of the twice born, the thread itself symbolizing the sun door, enabling the twice born to dwell in both time and in eternity.

Vibhuti, from a sachet in my briefcase. Fingers on the holy ash, swipe a broad stripe across the forehead. No shirt, just an angavastram around my shoulders. Eyes closed facing the mirror. Ten seconds silent prayer. Eyes open and traverse the reflection. Just this one day, I see myself as what I am. The true descendant of generations of priests in the temple town of Kumbakonam. A Brahmin in Brahmin garb.

* * *

The ritual of appeasing the departed soul is complex yet complete, as laid down in the Hindu religion. The premise of the ritual is that the soul roams free after death and is said to have attained Moksha, or eternal bliss, only when the prescribed rites are performed by the offspring. This and more I learned from the priest as the ceremony progressed.

By performing the ceremony, referred to as Shradh in the North and Shraddham in the South, the sons ensure that the dead continue to be looked after. I was surprised to know that the priests who partake in the ceremony actually are stand-ins. One priest represents the dead person, Pitru sthaan, the other is considered the witness, vishwa devar. A third priest represents Lord Vishnu.

Switching the sacred thread to the opposite side, I made offerings to the departed - til seeds, leaves of tulasi, balls of rice, and smearing of sandalwood paste.

Then, restoring the sacred thread to its rightful place on the right side of my chest, I made similar offerings, minus the til seeds, to the priest who was present as the witness, or saakshi as he is known. The ceremony lasted over an hour, after which the priest suggested that I partake food with a group of upcoming priests who had assisted him in chanting the mantras. It was sumptuous food, served traditional style on a banana leaf, with all the prescribed items that are normally served in a Shraddham meal – sweet balls of sesame seed, payasam made from jaggery and lentils, and appams stuffed with kesari and fried in ghee.

As I was preparing to leave, after thanking the group and handing over their due, dakshana as it is called, I asked the head priest if there was anything further I should do during the day.

"The ceremony is complete. From here on it is up to you… if you are free in the evening, you could visit a temple of your choice. You could perform an archana in God's name, or just the darshan is enough."

I asked Jambu for ideas. I suggested Kapaleeswarar Temple at Mylapore, Jambu suggested Vadapalani Temple, one of the biggest in Madras and 20 minutes drive from Chola. I asked him why, and he sheepishly explained that his daughter lived adjacent to the temple, and he would seize the opportunity to exchange notes with her, even if it was for 10 minutes. He said the temple opens at 4 pm, which meant that I had enough time to return to the hotel, and nap for two hours.

Refreshed with sleep and a cup of coffee, relieved that I had fulfilled my commitment to the departed soul, I entered the temple around 4.30 p.m. It was a Saturday evening, and was obviously a popular destination for worshippers in the area, for queues thronged the altar of every deity and people of all ages and social strata were moving around the perimeter. The main deity of the temple is Lord Muruga and at his sanctorum over a hundred people had gathered for the special pooja. The temple, I noted from a huge slab of engraved stone, was founded by one Periasamy Naicker, in whose dream Lord Muruga or Palani as he is also known, appeared and asked him to build a temple in the very place where the devotee lived. The shrine of Lord Muruga is located in six locations in Tamilnadu one of them is Palani, in the Southern Part of the State. The temple founded by Naicker, being in the Western part of the State came to be known as Vadapalani, Vadam being the word for the Westerly direction in Tamil.

I stood about 10 feet away from the sanctum sanctorum, observing the worshippers exiting from the pooja. I would go in when the crowd thinned out. I was in no particular hurry, and even while I idled, my mind was at work, reliving the most pulsating experience of my life - visit to the house of the chiffon girl, now known as Ranjini.

My mind marvelled her image in every replay, for such had been her presence and poise. Every trait of her personality had shone like diamonds studded in a necklace. Serene, controlled, subtle, yet expressive. Did I trace a sense of regret... longing... or was it just my imagination as usual. Probably regret that I had turned up, and longing for the husband to return home.

Oh, how fortunate her spouse is. Would those calm eyes light up when he returned from work? The warmth and affection she reserves for him, if I could receive for one glorious moment, I could spend the rest of my life savouring the ecstasy.

I had seen her yesterday after 20 years, I would never see her again. As my thoughts alternated between despair and disdain, my optical nerves were capturing a sight so extraordinary. Disbelief, total disbelief, as the nerves projected the image to the brain for verification. Call it chance, coincidence, destiny, or the mathematical probability of two people turning up at the same temple on a festive day. Or term it an incident so singular, it happens only once in one's life, when the person you are thinking of - appears in view.

Mrs. Ranjini Sudhakar. Moving gently, towards my general direction, but at a tangent, heading for the main deity. Her face calm, head slightly down, eyes traversing the ground, as befits the chaste Indian woman in a public place.

Her son and daughter were following a step behind. The three together to offer prayers, for the well being of the family. Perhaps the husband turning over a new leaf did not include piety.

Why this mark of favor? The Gods must have decided I had been too cynical, too remorseful and may be too provocative, almost obliquely challenging their power to put two people together at the most unexpected time and place.

Should I call out and announce my presence? Or go forward and claim her attention? Why was I standing rooted, and attempting to look away so as not to trigger her archetypal stimuli? I ransacked the brain for an answer... She was another man's wife, I had no place in her life. For her, I was a knight from the past, unwanted in the present. Logic warned that the warm and curious host of yesterday could turn cold and aloof today. She could interpret my presence as an act of pursuit, not happenstance. Better I remain the frog, she the fairy tale princess.

Cotton saree - the colour of orange peel, earrings like mini bells, no trace of make up, abundant black hair knotted in a single plait, no flowers. In every way, it was my lucky day. Unannounced, an angel had descended to give me the ultimate boon, of observing while remaining unobserved. I was happy to see her as she was, in a milieu in tune with her persona.

Reality, for those temporal moments that I held her in view, gave way to the surreal. As the seconds ticked, as she took every step, I could see no one but her. Even she, not in flesh and blood, but as a specter. Because, I was not looking at a person, but a lifelong dream.

Her children and she reached the main stupa, a 20 feet tall iron pillar about 15 feet from me. The three paused for a moment, and looked skyward at the gopuram, the temple tower which houses gods and demons in carvings above. From where I stood, I could lip read her instruction to the children to do a namaskaram, an essential ritual through which one salutes and thanks the deity. She passed her hand bag to her daughter and kneeled down as a Hindu woman would, and placed her hands on the ground, head bowed, staying in that position for a few seconds, perhaps praying for good health, happiness and long life, for her husband and children. I leaned back on a stone pillar and closed my eyes, fighting the tears and transmitting through sensory waves my best wishes. When I opened my eyes and wiped the tears, the family had left.

This silent encounter was so unique and unexpected, it would remain frozen in the subaltern caverns of my memory, within a forgotten space that treasures a few precious people and events. Such instances give me hope - that someday fate would deal a better card, not in its own time, but in a flash.

* * *

The next morning I went to the police headquarters to meet Inspector Kumaravel. I wanted to ask him to call off the search for the girl. I learned he had left with his men for security measures in the airport area, as the union minister who was likely to be arrested that afternoon lived in Nanganallur. The airport, CID reports revealed, would be picketed by his men if the arrest were to take place.

While leaving the hotel, while handing in the room key, I had noticed a counter in the lobby, set up by a mobile phone company, offering a handset on zero rent / deposit, with only airtime charged, an exclusive offer for the hotel's guests, apparently to promote their brand. On an impulse, I had taken a handset. I gave the junior my mobile number.

My mission had ended. I had one last visit, not within the mission parameters, but purely humanitarian. I wanted to visit Kasi Rao, my favourite waiter at Woodys. He would have grown old now. I wanted to check how he was faring, and whether he required monetary help.

Just once, when Kasi had been absent for two weeks because of his wife's terminal illness, I had visited his home in Nanganallur, at that time a fast-growing suburb near the airport. I asked Jambu to take me there.

We are self centered. We seldom realize it. Our goals, mission, duties, dreams and hopes take center stage in our life. We hardly notice minions around us who play minor but useful roles. With a sense of shame and self realization, I discovered while we were driving to Kasi Rao's home that I had not once asked Jambu a single personal detail. Very normal in the United States, but almost an insult in India where how curious you are benchmarks how concerned you are. Sure, Jambu had not asked either. But that gentle touch on my shoulder as I broke down at the school had been more soothing than balm on burn.

"How many years service, Jambu" I asked, ending my train of thoughts with a question. He fished out a cigarette pack from his shirt pocket, deftly lit up with both hands off the wheel, inhaled smoke and slowly exhaled the past from his heart.

"Started when I was 20, driving now for 30 years. My beat is airport to city, that too foreign flights. If passenger asks to come for duty, I go everywhere with him."

"Must have been different when you started work, I mean the airport."

"Oh, very different aiiya. We had a free run of the place those days. Once I even helped to change a puncture tire in a plane, Fakker Friend something they called it (he meant Fokker Friendship). Another time, I went with a pilot for a test ride also."

"How about passengers, you have more business now isn't it?"

"Yes sir, more planes, more passengers but also more taxis. Now 160 fellows. That time only 20 of us. We could go inside the luggage area those days. No conveyor belts and all. All suitcases the loaders will bring and keep on a large table. We drivers will be nearby. We pick out the passengers and say to ourselves: "Blue coat man for me, cooling glass madam for you, like that."

I wondered about his safety, and asked him if he was concerned driving into the city in the wee hours of the night.

"You mean if someone tries to rob me or take my taxi? Happened only once so far. I dropped passenger at Connemara, after that two fellows got in and tried to take my money."

"Oh really, anything happened to you?"

"Not to me," responded the veteran of a thousand nights on the road. "But they were in hospital for a week."

He cut speed, reached down to the floorboard with his left hand and pulled out from beneath the mat a mean cast iron rod. "It's always here. Same rod, 25 years."

* * *

As we neared the left turn to Nanganallur on the busy highway, my heart gave a tug as the idyllic, laid back old airport loomed ahead. From here, I had flown to a new life, leaving behind my mother and familiar surroundings.

"Stop, please stop, I mean go straight," the vocal chords crackled involuntarily, triggered by a wave of nostalgia. Jambu must have sensed

130

it was an impulse, for he slowed down, stopped the vehicle on the extreme left, and said without turning around:

"Where to Thambi, you want to go to the old airport?"

Darned right, I did. The driveway from the main gate and the single storey building that greeted us gave it a 60s aerodrome feel. I discovered the premises now housed the offices of cargo airlines. Cargo-laden aircraft take off from the airstrip, and at times those ferrying VIPs. I found Jambu's networking, from his years spent in the airport, was sufficient to get us through. He halted the taxi at the security cabin, alighted and spoke in drawling Tamil, studded with dialect, to the aging security head. He shared with me later that they both hailed from Tirunelveli district in Tamilnadu. They gave me a special pass, and Jambu was allowed to park within the premises, which he did in his usual spot of the days gone by.

The open lounge where the passengers would first enter, the bright red Avery weighing scales that would greet their luggage, the check in counter on one side, the airport manager's room, announcer's cabin and restaurant on the other, had disappeared. The atmosphere that had been charged with the novelty and luxury of air travel was absent. What greeted me were cabins and workstations, populated by people busy with their day's work. If I was a City Father, I would have campaigned for declaration of the place as an Heritage building, and restored the premises to its earlier state, to show future generations what airports were like in the old days. I was sorry to see one more landmark of old Madras change its facade.

There were boards all around, proclaiming the names of cargo and courier services – DHL, Elbee, Blue Dart and such, names that were not in my vocabulary when I had crossed that very lounge 20 years ago. With a tinge of sadness, I comprehended the change. Over time, the place must have been found inadequate to keep pace with the rise in passenger numbers and aircraft landings. Its infrastructure must have become obsolete and outdated to service the fly-by-wire jets and jet-setting passengers. Perhaps the relic had a message for me: Shape up or ship out.

Producing my pass to a security guard within, I proceeded towards the backend, to the area where the tarmac once commenced, to the place

131

where my mother had seen me off. I cannot recall her having said much, I remember her eyes doing the talking. Would she want to see me as I was today... rueful, morose and lonely?

The best tribute I could pay her, was change my melancholy self, change from a self-centered,. soul-searching human being to a society-aiding Good Samaritan.

Back to the taxi, and my assigned task. Guiding Jambu from memory, and making a few inquiries in a neighbourhood where everyone seemed to know everyone else, I found the placed where Kasi Rao lived, at Palavanthangal, near Nanganallur.

I feared he would not be home, for retired people tend not to remain at home. They can convert even an errand as a primary program of the day and opportunity for gainful activity. Say, a grandson has to be taken to the tailor, a retiree can turn it into a project, preparing, planning and meticulously executing the task. Not just errands, they are forever on the lookout for public meetings, social gatherings, award ceremonies, any event where legitimately they can spend time away from home and return at night with a satisfied "was very busy today" expression, much to the chagrin of the daughter in law who has to heat up food for the truant retiree. Not their fault really, but the failing of a society that ignores the inactive.

It was late in the afternoon. Only his daughter was at home. I spoke to her in the hall, the aroma of fresh coffee decoction wafting from within. I discovered Kasi Rao had left, of all places, for Woodys ten minutes earlier, for a very special reason.

"Today is the day he retired 15 years ago. And every year on this day, he goes there. He likes to sit around and watch the hustle and bustle of the hotel. For just a few hours, they allow him to work too. He puts on his white uniform, his starched cap, and attends to the tables." Her eyes were shining as she spoke, for she knew her father would cherish this annual opportunity to do what he loved most, serving customers who had come in to satiate their need for food and camaraderie.

I looked at the date on my watch. Jan.13, the day before Pongal Day. Seemed familiar. The date I visited Sowcarpet 20 years ago? No... how could I forget this date? It had been relevant like a birthday every year I had been away, but back in India, catching up with the past, rediscovering my roots, recovering from jet lag, and focussing on finding the girl, chronology had escaped my mind.

This date 20 years ago - jasmine, rejection, my forlorn walk around town, Woodys, and the first timer from WCC....

I knew that moment I wanted to be in Woodys. If time could not be reversed, if people could not be made to undo their misdeeds, at least one element was in my control. The power to place myself in a venue that resonated with my past. And reverse at least in my mind, the passage of time. If I could be seated at the same table, if Kasi Rao could serve me, if I could dwell on thoughts of my mother as though she were alive, if I could wonder what she had cooked for the evening and picture her happiness in serving me, for that fleeting moment I would get closer to my elusive goal.

"Jambu. Urgent. Cathedral Road, to Woodys, I mean the drive-in hotel."

"Saar, taking you to Mylapore, saar, Rayar's Café, good tiffin in the evening sir." He did not have to tell me about Rayar's, about their home style cooking, but this was not the time to explain.

"No, no, not for eating. Going for meeting."

Most of my life I have been afflicted by negative coincidences, or rather coincidences with negative impact. I take flowers to my aunt, and by sheer coincidence there's no family at home, and cousin screams. There's tension in town, and my father, not the 100 other officers, gets deputed for riot control. I visit my uncle in Colby, a fire starts, and my cousin and I end up alone. For the first time, life had handed out a decent deal. Kasi Rao retires on the day I met her, Jan. 13, and 20 years later I visit his home on the same date. Just proves that whatever will be, will be.

Another coincidence, rather a harsh repeat of history, awaited me, two minutes ahead on the road. We had just crossed the polo grounds on our left, when we noticed commotion ahead. A group of protesters waving placards and shouting slogans had gathered in the middle of the road. Vehicles were coming to a halt on both sides. I had no time for local problems, local politics. "Quick Jambu, take a side street, towards OTS side, you can drive through the army area and exit at Guindy."

Jambu seemed to nod in appreciation of my local knowledge, and swung left at the turn just before we could be stopped by what is popularly known and oft practiced in India - rasta roko.

We turned left and immediate right, and drove onward for about two minutes. That's when we saw what we often read about in Indian newspapers but never encounter face to face. "Stop the taxi, stop," I cried frantically.

* * *

CHAPTER NINE

"The adventure of the hero represents the moment in his life when he achieved illumination - the nuclear moment when, while still alive, he found and opened the road to the light beyond the dark walls of our living death."

Three hoodlums were dousing a stationary public bus, a ladies special, with kerosene. The bus must have taken the short cut too, and had been trapped in the solitary road. The bus had around 10 women and a few children in it and the goondas were preventing them from alighting. The driver and conductor were not to be seen.

We screeched to a halt next to the bus. I sprang out and ran to the footboard at the front where a local thug was brandishing a knife. Another had blocked the rear entrance, arms akimbo.

"You want to burn the bus, do it," I said. "But let the passengers go. You cannot harm them."

See, see, someone has come from the sky to speak law. Yow, poyya, do you want to leave this place alive?"

He did not know I had no interest in living. I had nothing to look forward to in life, except retracing my past and relishing childhood memories. We were running out of time, two ruffians had completed dousing the bus and returned with empty jerry cans. The women were pleading to be let out, frantically waving their hands out of the windows, realizing that the thugs were actually carrying out their threat. From the corner of my eye, I could see a man emerging from a hut and running towards the group, holding a burning stick of firewood.

That was the kicker. In a country where citizens resort to violence to express their differences over language, religion, caste and politics, where taking another's life is the most brutal form of sending a message to the State, the protester deserves no mercy. My father was right in taking five people with his revolver. If he had a battle tank, he would have taken the whole lot.

135

All the negative energy bottled up in me, all the hate I had stored against anti-social elements, all the vengeance I had harboured against them, erupted in that millisecond when I saw the burning piece of wood. Because I, more than anyone else, knew the significance of the torching of people who had no reason to die. When the legal system takes so much care before awarding the final capital punishment, in terms of opportunity for appeals, clemency and presidential pardon, how can we allow individuals to execute the innocent summarily!

Life changes in just a few seconds. All it takes is the right trigger, igniting a change so powerful, so intense and incisive, that the change is forever. It must have happened to me as I watched the lungi-clad activist emerging from the hut, carrying the harbinger of death to those in the bus. It was as though decades later in time, my father's DNA was destined to witness the gruesome repeat of history: burning of the living by a fellow human being. I knew then I had to protect the women and children, because the command was embedded in my genes. My time had come, to live honourably or die in the line of duty.

And at that divine moment, when the Lord announces your true station, when he proclaims you as the protector, the heaven above and ground below give you one monumental chance to prove yourself, when you win over fear, pain and the prospect of death. At that supreme state of inward clarity, on that heightened emotional plane, I experienced an oracle: the unshackling of my past, unravelling to the mind's eye the greatest folly of my life: folly of inaction.

Never again would my life be dotted with situations of "would have" and "should have." Never again would I look back, lament the past. I would act, in the present. My father had acted, and died honourably.

I am ready for self-annihilation. I can hear the harmonious acclaim of the Gods of the heavens, as they gather to observe my atonement. I am no longer a man but a hero who has penetrated beyond life and source, to the supreme void where darkness is light.

Three hooligans with knives closing in around me. Ten seconds before the burning piece of wood is thrown at the bus. Now or never. My clubbed knuckles crashed into the jaw of the nearest man, taking him by surprise. Next, a violent kick on the stomach of another, causing him to double up in pain. The third backs off a step, unsure now whether I am a maniacal savior or a trained army commando. In that split second, I race towards the flamethrower, running into him with all my 160 pounds. The firewood slips off his hand as we crash into the ground. I want to batter these law breakers into pulp. I have no fear. I am a Kshatriya in Brahmin garb.

"Thambi! Catch!" the voice of Jambu from 30 feet away, as I get back on my feet faster than anyone else. Thousands of miles of road running, years of rigorous exercise and pumping iron. A lifetime of smouldering within. Time to unleash anger, frustration and bottled emotions. Iron rod sailing through the air into my hands, as the hooligans regroup. Power flowing from my shoulders into wrists. Swinging the rod "silambu" style, the way my father would do with a stick. Thud, thud, thud, the sound of metal crashing into flesh and bone. Blood spilling from torn cheeks and scalps, cries of pain rending the air.

Put the rioter at risk.

* * *

En route to Woodys some 20 minutes later. Refreshed with a splash of water from a bottle Jambu carried in the dashboard. Spruced up by running a comb through my hair, and dusting my clothes at his insistence.

Mind and body strangely light, the upshot of extreme stress, extreme relief. Old events suddenly visible in a new light. Revisit of truths to check for lies lurking within. And in a flash, the truth about the girl, nay woman, revealed. A streak of suspicion that had emanated 20 years ago. as the auto trundled past Mylapore Pharmacy, now affirmed.

Cold and self-serving? You bet. I had meant nothing to her. It was time to end a chapter, and exit from a wasteland I had wandered in for 20 years. Time for the final escape from the gnarled lanes in the labyrinth of my mind.

Time for my reunion with Woodys, and with Kasi Rao, the last kind soul in this world. The black and yellow taxi swung into the tree-lined driveway, drove past the scattering of cars in the car park and took a U turn, halting at the flame of the forest tree. I alighted and entered the restaurant, exactly after 20 years.

If there was a spot to step back in time, there could have been no better choice. Because, nothing, I mean nothing had changed. The restaurant, and the self-service section looked no different from the last time I had been here. Even the little shop at the corner of the restaurant, where I bought toffees and the others cigarettes, was unchanged. I had been a regular visitor for almost four years, but did not expect to be recognized in an institution that caters strictly to retail customers whose names and faces fade with the passage of time. I was mature enough to know that while I treasured the nooks and corners, for the hotelier I was just another guest. In a sense, the institution was like a celebrity about whom one knows every detail, but not the other way around.

I chose the farthest table in a discreet corner. My back to the clientele, soaking in the ambience, nurturing memory recall, to the same day, two decades ago. Frowning at the jasmine encounter. Savouring the image of the girl as she walked past me by the tree. The warm glow that lingered even after she was out of sight. I had done everything right after that, saved her from trouble, dropped her home. Twenty years too late, I wished I had come back the next day into her life. If she could accept Sudhakar, she would have welcomed me. The trouble with women was, you never knew.

I was brought back to the present by a plate of gulab jamun being placed on the table. Trust Kasi Rao to know my mood. I was pensive, but relaxed, so it called for indulgence. "Thank you Kasi, I will have coffee a little later," I said this as casually as I could, without looking up, as I had many times during the four years. But the moment was too strong to retain as a make-believe of the past. I rose and hugged the old man, tears flowing from two pairs of eyes. The past never comes back, but people do.

"Chinnayya, how are you? How many years since I saw you last? Let me not disturb you; eat your sweet. I have to serve two more tables, then I will come back."

He came back a few minutes later with two cups of coffee. Seated together like old friends, we spent a pleasant few minutes exchanging notes. "So, this place hasn't changed at all, Kasi," I said, filled with nostalgia.

"Engappa, nobody comes here. Those golden days are gone. The college girls, and boys who came here, around your time… now, they have gone to what is it called, cyber cafes - that internet, chatting and all that. No one talks face to face any more. No one values people and friendships in this day and age…" he rambled on.

I did not want Kasi Rao to talk of the present. He did not belong to it. I would have been content even if he did not talk.

"I will tell you something, Chinnayya,. I never forget dates. I retired on this date, as my daughter would have told you, but this date has some relevance for you also. You may not remember, but an old man like me never forgets."

"What is it?" I asked absently, expecting him to come up with something irrelevant. He had no reason to know the relevance I placed on this date.

"Remember the girl one evening? You almost got into a fight. You led her out of the hotel. In fact, I never saw you again after that. Remember that girl?"

"Oh, that incident. Been a long time, long back, but I do remember. What about it?"

"Every year on the same day, she comes here, at the same time, alone. For last the 20 years. I know… because today is the day."

Goose bumps. Clutch of the heart. Color draining from my face. My world turns upside down; the mind fights for equilibrium, looking for reasons, meaning, anything to make sense of her repetitive action. Why? And why not tell me when I visited her? When would I understand women?

"Today, has she come and gone?" Casual tone, but too casual for a man who had spent his life interacting with people.

"She is there, right now, on the self service side. Go, talk to her."

I headed towards the shop, bought a toffee, unwrapped it slowly, just as I had, at the same spot 20 years ago. Life's greatest moments can happen so fast, so unexpectedly. She was seated at the same table. Past evolved into present, present yearned for the past. We are never alone in wanting to turn the clock back.

Just then, my mobile phone beeped, the modern gadget jarred and broke the magic spell. I had wanted to draw up a chair and ask a classic question: "Been waiting for long?"

I did not know how to switch the ringer off. I took the call by pressing the green key. Must be the phone company asking if I had found the phone useful, and reception clear.

"I am busy now, please call later," I snapped.

"I say, Arjun, this is Uncle Kumaravel. Listen. I called to tell you not to move around too much in town. We have arrested a political leader, his followers are creating trouble. They tried to burn a bus near OTS. An army chap, we are trying to find out who he is, managed to beat the hell out of the hooligans. Get back to your hotel and stay there, I don't want you to get hurt, OK?"

The moment was too precious to be interrupted, that too with stale news. "All right uncle, I will take care," I said curtly.

"Hey, don't hang up, now that you are on the line, one more piece of information," the inspector continued to my dismay. "Remember the woman you asked me to trace? We found the address... she lives in Anna Nagar. But don't go there. Not the right time."

A sense of foreboding crept over me. Something she had said to her son, something she had not said to me.

"Have you copied all the portions from Rahul, whatever you missed during the last two weeks?"

Something hidden from the five senses, but perceptible to the sixth. An understated, hidden truth that I, in my self-centered state had overlooked.

"The union staff came last week."

"Don't go there for some days. Her husband, nice guy, I believe. He had a chequered past, but corrected his ways after he married her.

"Her husband..." the inspector continued: "He died in a boiler blast at his factory around two weeks ago."

* * *

140

CHAPTER TEN

The call rings up the curtain, always, on a moment of spiritual passage,
which when complete, amounts to dying or birth.

I asked for a transfer to India, the week after the fracas near OTS
and the call from Kumaravel. I had spent many years in the backend,
supervising the team that would store and run the data. Now, I wanted
to be in the field, to interact with the people whom Neel Akash had
pledged to assist. I wanted to work closely with the lawyers and NGOs
we fund from overseas. I no longer shun people, I will no longer stick
to my cocoon, I have the courage to face the world. I want to reach out,
and touch the lives of others, in my own humble way.

On a personal level, I am closely involved with my mother's alma
mater. I had created a generous endowment from my savings, and a
portion of this was deployed to educate six orphan children.

The truth was, I wanted to do much more for these children, students
of the school where my mother had studied 50 years ago. To make up for
what my mother had lost in her school days. Educational tours, picnics
and excursions. Decent footwear, books, money to buy them.

I live in an apartment two blocks away. My greatest joy is my morning
routine. Finish my run, and around 8 a.m. arrive at the school gate, to
hear the morning clamor, and take in one of the world's greatest sights:
Scores of children milling around the brick and mortar, well clothed,
fed and cared for. That's the best gift you can give a needy child, the gift
my mother missed.

I try not to think of her childhood, but picture her among the children
50 years later, satchel in hand and a smile on her lips.

I follow an unusual practice. I take the orphan children to my
ancestral home on Saturdays where we spend the weekend together. I
want them to experience what a real home is. I like hovering around
them like a father figure. It is role play, more true than the false roles
many play in real life.

We have a meal together in the dining room, sit around and watch TV just like any other family on Saturday night. My eyes turn misty when I put them to bed, draw the sheet and put off the light. I sleep down in the hall, with memories of my mother and father.

* * *

Rekha Sen caught up with me at Chola the day after I saw Ranjini at Woodys. Naturally, I brought her up to date on recent events. She was saying something about a mannath, and about feeding 500 orphans in Calcutta. I guess she must have got a plum role as an answer to a prayer.

Neelam sent me an email last week, in response to my detailed mail, saying she was happy to learn of my progress. She had mailed on her official e-letterhead, and I feel sheepish when I recall the inscription. I realise, with wry self-deprecation, that we should not slot people into a stereotype. While I work for an organization that attempts to change how the world looks at women, I have to work harder to follow these ideals in my own life.

Dear Arjun... began her email:

I derived immense professional satisfaction from our frequent inter-actions, especially the interactive session at my apartment and the extraordinary exchange of views at the lake. I don't know how to say this, but your innocence is enchanting. Beyond a point, you were not a patient but a soul mate. Your demure attitude helped balance my extrovert manner. Your unswerving sense of morality reinforced my belief that in a world of cowards, a few good men still exist. If I had expressed a need to be closer to you, emotionally and physically, the desire was spurred by your hesitation, by the human quest for forbidden fruit.

Let me confess to what you know by now: I am a psychiatrist, though not a very good one.

Well, that's enough said about me...

From the numerous incidents you have shared with me, including the recent happenings in Madras, and from the cultural backdrop you have described earlier, permit the professional in me to enumerate the sociological triggers that prompted specific actions and reactions from you and the other central characters in your life.

First, let's take the city of Madras, the prime canvas in our proscenium theatre. The most impressionable moments in your life happened in the 70s, a time when morality was at its peak in Madras. Yet, with its attendant incongruities: For the pubescent, for women like Ranjini, it was a period when emotions stood contained, words remained unsaid and feelings restrained. Men like you, when coming of age were swayed by the gender's genetic fascination for femininity, yet your overt expression of admiration was often hindered by cultural impasse.

People part of your social fabric are a product of the times; reflex to crisis a reflection of moral fiber. Their beliefs and severity of views may seem puritan and archaic; yet for women such as Ranjini and Nirupama, diametric shades of black and white, were natural and acceptable. Grey would be a compromise.

This tranquil society could not remain unaltered for long. Over time it has been sullied... by invasion, migration and imposition of contrarian beliefs, and the trauma of re-engineering has surfaced across moral and social platforms in this quiet, unhurried and conservative city. The old guard has witnessed time and again, symbols of change that signal the funeral of order, the diffident shuffle of pallbearers, and dreads the catharsis that may soon wreck their value systems.

offer these words as a palliative for you and many others who tend to cling to the old order. From the naiveté of the 60s, today we experience a new pragmatism in the 90s. Every decade in these 30 years has been a juxtaposition of transient phases, each marking the passing of familiar forms. The late 70s heralded the first signs of crumbling, of the walls of propriety, revealing a harsh and unfamiliar world.

Now let's switch to my favourite subject... you. I learnt soon something very interesting about you: For you, the present offers little that is precious. Because the clock cannot be put back, you constantly rewind your mind, savouring a rich brew of memories, reviving the times gone by, forever seeking your holy grail – reunion with the woman whom you had met just once.

Your problems are Freudian. You suffer from infantile affect, from excessive attachment to the world of childhood. Your unconscious has not fully severed its umbilical ties. You often summoned for solace your earliest embedded memory – crawling up the stairs to your mother's warm arms - when demons of the present tormented your mindscape.

In a typical life cycle, the human being establishes himself as an independent person, and secures a job and mate. This independence requires the mastery of one's instincts, and rerouting them into socially acceptable outlets. Sexual desire gets rerouted from one's mother to a mate, or redirected into non-erotic love or art. The instinct of aggression may be sublimated into competition.

In many ways, in thought and deed, you transcended the typical, and elevated your life from humdrum to extraordinary. You gave vent to aggression by competing with yourself, through strenuous physical exertion. You often adopted a fatalistic view of anguish. On the dark side, you believed smudges in your youth to be indelible stains. I discovered every facet and pieced them together, and these when put together with your departure from Madras and subsequent return gave rise to a pattern that is marvelled in psychology: the mystical hero's journey, and its

144

attendant rites of passage – separation, initiation, departure, fulfillment
and return.

My apologies for probing your mind without disclosing my domain.

Best wishes,

Dr. Neelam Gupta, M.D.
(Royal College of Psychiatry, London)

* * *

I am getting to know Ranjini better. She said she had come to Woodys a month later and asked around for me, just to thank me once again. She did not say this, but even my brain, normally slow when it comes to women, deduced that my physical absence made my presence all the more vital, because as days passed, she felt more and more guilty for having adopted a "Don't come back into my life attitude." And the only way she could make amends was to meet me face to face. She said she came every year on the same date and time to find me, leaning on the Indian psyche of marking anniversaries.

I asked her what prompted her to visit the temple with the children, and also keep her annual appointment at the restaurant, just two weeks after her husband's death. Her explanation was enlightening. According to Hindu rites, the period of mourning ends on the 13th day. From the very next day, she was determined to lead a normal life, not for her benefit, but for her children. With the calamity behind, she was determined to give them the appearance of normality, and this was a drastic but necessary demonstration of her resolve. Lastly, when I wondered why she did not divulge news of her husband's passing when I came home, her reply was astounding yet rational. It is our culture, she explained, to welcome a visitor, even one who arrives unannounced, or unaware of circumstances at home.

She recalled the story in Hindu mythology, in which God, who had arrived in the form of a guest, was being served a meal on a leaf while the son lay dead in the backyard, bitten by a snake while cutting the very leaf from the tree. Her replies revealed a part of her that I wished I had known two decades ago.

I admire her not just because she is beautiful, but for qualities she has demonstrated during crises – steadfastness, perseverance, an ability to restore balance by drawing on a stored resolve, and an inner steel that concealed her emotions. Had we been a pair, she would have helped offset my inaction, deferment and constant brooding with her strength of character.

* * *

Rekha Sen wrote to me in August, conveying the success of her comeback vehicle on the silver screen, an unusual black and white film set in the 50s, a no frills venture completed in just 30 days, directed by a debutant. She had sent me the press reviews, interviews and a few CDs too. I was so impressed with the film that I couriered a CD to Neelam, raving about Rekha Sen. Her reply was tepid, acknowledging she had viewed the CD, and suggesting Ms. Sen should look for roles that suit her age. I passed on a copy to Ranjini, extolling the virtues of the actress on screen and off it; she didn't seem too thrilled either. I guess women will glower when a man gushes over another woman.

* * *

Come September, the children came to me with an unusual appeal. They had seen a cluster of dolls when I had been rummaging in the attic and had been curious to play with them. I had explained that these were not playthings but dolls designated for Kolu, a nine-day festival that features replicas of deities and humans. Would I agree, asked the children, to organize Kolu for them? Could they help, could they invite their friends from school? Arjun Anna, would you please say yes?

I hesitated, knowing the anchor of such a festival, a woman, was absent in my life. Diffidence gave way to acceptance, for the sake of the children.

Kolu brings back a treasure of memories. Standing in the empty hall on the day before, I recalled from folklore and family tales the significance of Navrathri and the accompanying Kolu display.

Navaratri, which means nine nights, is observed for nine days from the day after the new moon and ends with a festival named Vijayadasami. If I remember right, the first three days are dedicated to Durga, the vanquisher of evil. The next three days to Lakshmi, the Goddess who confers prosperity. The last three days to Saraswathy the Goddess of learning.

My mother would say the dolls personify the divine. The specific arrangements she would make for the exhibition never changed – a magnificent display on seven or nine ascending steps made from wooden planks, and placed on angular steel brackets. The steps would be covered with white cloth. The topmost step would house dolls of Ganesa, Durga, Lakshmi, Saraswati, the Trinity, the incarnations of Vishnu and Radha and Krishna together. There would also be thematic exhibits such as a temple festival, a marriage in progress or a large kitchen at work. I know we had a pot bellied merchant, a washer man, three policeman dolls to humour my father, busts and small statues of Gandhi, Nehru and Bose. The bottom-most step had replicas of vegetables plus a deer, two elephants and a lion. The steps would be decorated elaborately with serial lights, and on the ground we would have a moving display of a toy train.

We started a week in advance. The dolls, wrapped in cotton rags and neatly stacked in huge wooden crates, were carefully taken out, dusted, mended and given a fresh coat of paint. One evening, we went together to Mylapore, to the shops alongside the temple tank, to buy more dolls - a Ramayana set, a Dasavatara set and a set of musicians, and a miniature kitchen — various utensils made of brass, which were filled with a few grams of grains and pulses.

We went together to Marina beach and brought a bucket of sand. We gathered clay from the playground opposite, to lay a village scene, with sand strewn for the roads. We made a mini-temple of clay, with an imposing tower, and placed it on a small hillock. Using a brass trough, we created a mud tank in front of the temple.

We invited Ranjini and her children. My aunt and uncle and cousin from West Mambalam. The school teachers and parents. For the little organizers, it was a nine-day lesson in discipline, courtesy and relationship-building. For me a pandering to an ingrained yearning, deglutinating an ever-lasting desire to resurrect and restore the child within.

On the last day of the nine-day Navrathri festival, the children and

I assembled to perform a reluctant but obligatory task: dismantle the steel racks, remove the wooden planks, pack the colorful serial lights and the dolls.

I recalled the order in which the dolls had to be stowed in the attic. The earthen, painted dolls first, each wrapped in cloth and hay, followed by the wax-molded Hindu deities and finally the assortment of miniatures from the bottom-most rack. As the last of the dolls passed from hand to hand, and up a wooden ladder into their designated space in the attic, as the evening shadows descended on the skylight, the conclusion of the festivity became certain. Initial exuberance gave way to remorse. Silence engulfed the work environment. There was nothing more to stow but the memories.

The youngest child broke into tears, the older ones gathered around me with downcast eyes, seeking consolation, compassion and restoration of a sense of purpose. I beckoned them to come closer, and hugged them tight, my outstretched arms encircling at least four. At that very moment, the physical bonding and emotional attachment must have enabled a transference of innocence, a simplicity of thought that dwells in us only during childhood. A fresh clarity dawned, not one as severe and sudden as the revelation sparked by the flamethrower, but through an emotion kinder and gentler, which in the days to come, could help resolve my constant conflicts with the past.

I realized at that moment the dolls served as a metaphor, and the act of putting them away symbolized the storage of memories in the safe repository of my heart. The stowage signified that the past would, and should never go away. Yet, the period can be wrapped and returned to where it belongs, in the attic of our soul, where memories of yore and yonder, of people and places, dwell in peace and harmony. The mystical helpers of our childhood reside within, and when we seek that which is lost, elfins, pixies and goblins emerge from the safe depository to revive the romance of the nursery, rekindling the gentle rock of the cradle, while embedded voices whisper a lullaby, restoring the mind from eternal toil to ephemeral rest.

* * *

Mahabalipuram beach, 45 km from Chennai, formerly Madras.

"*Pasangala*, last one minute. Quick, quick," the voice of my personal driver - Jambu. The children are building sand castles. All in a row. Three to a team. I have given them water, a mini spade, and five minutes to build the tallest and most creative castle. I have not revealed my hopes to Ranjini - but I build my own sandcastles.

Circumstances of the recent past compel me ponder the imponderable, and wonder if a change is inclined in a pre-charted destiny. Just as the Lord was forced to acknowledge the devotion of Markandeya and declare he would live forever rather than die at the age of sixteen, I wonder whether the efficacy of my devotion is determining a change in his Will. Is it for this reason I have been summoned after so long to my homeland, is it the reason for her husband to be called now to the world above?

A converse phenomenon deserves mention. Diverse cultures across the world have commonalities. In the realm of love, hate and human bonding, they reflect established universal truths. However advanced you may term a culture, in the institution of marriage, it often holds the "first" dear. It is the first husband or first wife who has a special place. If the spouse were to die prematurely, the next person is always compared with the previous. I did not want to be in that slot. They had lived as husband and wife for over 10 years. They would have shared inner hopes, fears and fantasies. Knowing her background, knowing her as only I could, I knew she would have remained faithful to her husband when he was alive. How would she be unfaithful in his absence? I understand and appreciate that.

My logic, clear as it may be, does not overrule the heart. Deep within, it will always resonate the unspoken words. She cannot hear it, the inner voice of a man who loves a woman dearly and forever.

If marriage completes life, and if I wish to test that premise, the only option would be to seek the hand of another. I won't, because I will look for Ranjini in every woman. If not her, I will be stoic as my culture has taught to be, and let it be.

* * *

The schoolteachers are a few metres away, taking a roll call, to ensure

149

no one is left behind. The headmistress is at my side. "We are lucky to have you as our patron, Mr. Arjun, you have made so much difference to the school and to the life of these children," she is saying. I nod, as is the Indian habit when addressed by a person of stature, and quickly shake my head, in a gesture of humility, as is the Indian habit.

As the waves pound and ebb, as the children and others gather their belongings and head to the bus, as Jambu recedes to the car to leave me alone, I mull over the irony of her statement. How do I explain that it is my life that has changed, with this involvement? Accepting the acclaim of a savior and acknowledging my support as sacrifice would be blasphemy, because I am the beneficiary, not a donor.

The children bring me happiness, make me feel emotionally secure. They are my calling, caring for them is my karma. By a hand of fate, they are a valuable possession entrusted to my custody. In finding them, I have found my station in life. Ranjini, will be my guiding light, perhaps never the destination. She is my North Star, the children my lodestar.

* * *

150

CHAPTER ELEVEN

In the vocabulary of the mystics, this is the second stage of the Way, that of the purification of the self, when the senses are cleansed and humbled... this is the process of dissolving... the infantile images of our personal past.

Water lapping at my feet. Sun sinking in the sea. Sky turning angry grey. Catamaran carrying home the catch. No one else on the beach. Mind retracing events of the recent past: Signs and tokens, metaphors and symbols, milestones in a mystical journey that led to a metamorphism within.

Retracing my mother's footsteps helped satiate a primal desire to return to the root of one's roots. In Arumugham's anguish, expressed in a sob overheard, I found proof that you can escape the law but not justice. The obsolete airport taught me I would have to keep pace with the present, or turn into a relic.

I no longer look at life in duality, as a pair of opposites – right and wrong, ethical and unethical, good and evil. With this learning, if there is one thing I would go back and change, it is, strangely, resisting Neelam at the lake. Not to justify lust, but to beautify a natural impulse, sublimate a spontaneous emotion.

Ranjini's visits to the restaurant conveyed more than the marking of an anniversary – a gratifying truth that the person I had wanted most, wanted me. Culture, circumstances and an inherent introversion had stalled her from crossing the threshold. Hence, the subtle, annual ritual.

At my uncle's home in the USA, walking out when Nirupama relived her trepidation, liberated me from caring about those who are insensitive and incapable of change. The custom of stowing dolls taught me to unshackle and let go. Like the dolls asleep in the attic, the past is now at rest.

The crucial turning point, the ultimate transformation of

consciousness, was near the OTS, when I had to make a choice: live for myself, or die for others. It was an overwhelming psychological experience of death, resurrection and illumination. A spiritual ordination that earned me the right to lead, and transmit the light to others.

The upshot of my experiences is that I am now beyond temporal apparitions. I am no longer compelled by desire or fear. I have buried hatred, and every other hatchet.

As a solitary seagull glides overhead, I fish out a book of poems from a satchel, a gift from the Class 2 teacher. I had expressed a wish to see the collection, still part of the curriculum after 50 years. Pages, memories of mother flutter in the breeze. Heart misses a beat. Her progeny reads the full poem, 50 years later.

The Little Plant

In the heart of a seed,

Buried deep, oh, so deep

A dear little plant

Lay fast asleep

Wake said the sunshine

And creep to the light

Wake said the voice

Of the rain drops bright

The little plant heard

And it rose to see

Oh, how wonderful

The world might be!

There is no note on this page, but her Std. 9 scribble is fresh in my mind: *Give me hope, give me faith, give me a good husband whom I can love till my very end... Give me a child who will give other children what I do not have.*

152

"I will, Amma, I will do my best," I promise aloud. Waves cheer, thunder claps, rain drops fall on my head, like rice in a religious ceremony.

The best things in life can't be told, but can be found scribbled in a schoolbook. I know at that moment that the little good I do for these children is the fulfilment of a pre-natal wish, written in my genes long before I was born. She had willed it in her, carried the wish in her gene. My destiny must have been charted on those verses, as she read and perhaps read them again while putting her books away for the last time.

The raindrops turn from pitter-patter to a sharp shower. Pure, fresh water jets from the pregnant clouds above. Millions of gallons of saline in the seascape ahead.

Hundreds of miles above, somewhere in the stratosphere, in that part of the cosmos reserved for the departed to roam free, two celestial beings witnessing the solemn ceremony below. The Shraddham of a man's past, performed by the rain gods.

Kumaramangalam and Marakatham bless their offspring from above. The departed souls know what we don't. That rites do not suffice. Only when loved ones resolve inner conflicts and radiate happiness, can the spirits above rest in peace.

* * *

Nothing now remains. Demons exorcised, the guilty punished, insult redeemed, poem complete. Like the little plant, I rise to see the wonderful world.

END

ACKNOWLEDGEMENTS

I wrote my first short story 20 years ago. Seven more followed in the next 12 years. Sometime, somewhere, I knew I was ready for a novel. The genesis was a poem in my daughter's school book… In the heart of a seed, buried deep, oh, so deep, a dear little plant lay fast asleep. All I did was water the seed and bring the plant to life.

North Star was written over a period of three years. I put the manuscript away for the next four years, then fished it out and fleshed out many of the scenes. I knew the story was not complete in the first draft... some of the characters had to receive their due.

The visit of Arjun to the Minister's house, and the meeting with Constable Mathivanan on his death bed, had to be penned, as the final tribute to Inspector Kumaramangalam. The anguish of Arjun, of being misunderstood by Nirupama, had to be played out more and more, until all the angst was wrung out through his words and actions.

I have a lot to thank for in the writing of this book: A home environment conducive to creativity, and tolerant of my pensive moods. Being in advertising has been a blessing; years of experience in encapsulating an entire company or brand in a terse headline and crisp body copy helped me say more with less.

My background as a short story writer has affected, nay shaped, the flow of the novel. You would notice no scene is too long, no chapter is long drawn out; characters make quick entries, time periods morph into another and take you back and forth, story threads run concurrently and help bind characters, while sub plots softly blend and steer the protagonist towards the final resolution.

Support from several quarters has made the novel come true:

- Kala, Chandni and Vignesh – your encouragement has been my elixir.

- Ashok Mittal and Malathi Mittal – for the sojourns at your cottage in Coonoor. Fireside chats in your living room that lead to meaningful critique, and your warm hospitality which is a writer's dream come true.

-   Neela Mazumdar and Rakhi Purnima Dasgupta for their insight into Kolkata, and Bengali culture.

-   Asst. Commissioner K. Shanmugam, (Retd.) for sharing information in the public domain on police training and techniques of investigation.

-   Dr. Kanchana Srinivasan for her inputs on psychology and analysis of the central character.

-   N.V. Prakash, the real-life son of slain inspector Venkatesh, for reliving those painful moments of the anti-Hindi agitation.

-   V. Ramnarayan, for his editing. If you think you know English, he makes you eat humble pie with his eye for detail and precise corrections.

-   To my publishers, Thinkbigbooks, specifically the director - publishing, Divya Mardia, for approaching a literary work scientifically, making structured decisions at every step of the process.

-   To M.U. Narendran for the nostalgic wrapper design, with a yesteryear photograph that gives a whiff of what's within.

The mesmerizing quotes that precede each page are excerpts from "The Hero with a Thousand Faces," by Joseph Campbell.

R. Chandramouli
August
2009